D1384803

ALL THAT GLIMMERS

Marlene Chase

Annie's®
AnniesFiction.com

Books in the Secrets of the Quilt series

All That Glimmers
Copyright © 2016, 2018 Annie's.

All rights reserved. No part of this publication may be reproduced, stored in a re-
trieval system, or transmitted in any form or by any means—electronic, mechani-
cal, photocopying, recording or otherwise—without the prior written permission
of the publisher. The only exception is brief quotations in printed reviews. For
information address Annie's, 306 East Parr Road, Berne, Indiana 46711-1138.

The characters and events in this book are fictional, and any resemblance to actual
persons or events is coincidental.

Library of Congress-in-Publication Data
All That Glimmers / by Marlene Chase
p. cm.
I. Title
                    2016942654

AnniesFiction.com
(800) 282-6643
Secrets of the Quilt™
Series Creator: Shari Lohner
Series Editors: Shari Lohner, Janice Tate, and Ken Tate
Cover Illustrator: Jonathan Bouw

10 11 12 13 14 | Printed in China | 9 8 7 6 5 4 3

1

Kanesville, Iowa
April 1849

Adelia Long straightened the black folds of her bombazine dress. Three weeks of mourning for Papa had not dulled the pain of his absence or the dread news that had come to her and her younger brother, Quinton. To add to her misery, a familiar carriage drove up to the house. A visit from Uncle Edward hardly promised good things. She braced herself and slowly opened the front door.

"Good afternoon, Adelia. I trust my coming does not inconvenience you." Edward Long gripped his black hat in plump fingers over his waistcoat. "Felicity would have accompanied me, but the dear soul is in the throes of one of her headaches."

"My sympathies to Aunt Felicity," Adelia managed with difficulty. Her aunt, who bore little resemblance to her pleasant-sounding name, enjoyed frequent bouts of illness.

"It is I who extend my deepest condolences," Edward said, bowing slightly and pursing wet lips.

Adelia indicated the best chair in the small parlor of the home where she, Papa, and Quinton had lived for as long as Adelia could remember. She waited for her uncle to settle his considerable bulk in the chair.

Adelia had been twelve when her mother died, succumbing only days after the fever set in. For the past thirteen years, she

5

had kept house for Papa and Quinton, now the sole proprietor of the hardware store Horace Long had owned. She felt her throat constrict, recalling her father's quick smile and gentle brown gaze. With him, she had felt safe, assured that nothing bad could ever happen.

Papa was compassionate and hardworking but nonetheless something of a failure in business, a fault that did not go unnoticed or unremarked on by Uncle Edward. The Long family largely looked on Horace with pity and some disdain. After all, he'd married the daughter of a poor seamstress who'd left him a widower, a stroke of ill fate. Now, he, too, was dead, and solicitors confirmed that after paying off his debts, his two children would be in dire straits financially.

"I've come to offer more than sympathy, my dear," Edward went on, leaning forward on the last well-upholstered chair in the parlor. He had grown more portly in recent years, and his thinning hair had faded to a gunmetal gray. He cleared his throat. "I'm aware of your, shall we say, unfortunate circumstances."

He paused, casting sharp eyes over the spare parlor. Adelia had sold off what furniture they could do without. Turning his gaze back to her, he wagged his head as if contemplating something that puzzled him. "May I inquire first of all, my dear, if you have given thought to reconsidering your friendship with Hiram Powell?"

She lowered her head to hide her irritation, first at the intrusion into her private affairs and second at his implication that she should marry the well-placed widower simply because she had no alternative. Hiram had been seeking a replacement for his dead wife for some time and had recently taken notice of Adelia. Of course, she knew that women in her circumstances had few options and little means of support outside of marriage.

"If you please, Uncle," she began, setting her jaw and clenching her hands in her lap. "I'm grateful for your kind interest, but I do not wish to be constrained to such a union. I—" She stopped, for she could think of no way to explain herself adequately.

It wasn't that she hadn't thought about accepting Hiram—he was a good man who would no doubt provide for her adequately—but to think of living every day with a man who failed to touch her soul in any way was abhorrent. She swallowed hard. She was no prize, she knew. Her mouth was too big, and she possessed none of the curly locks bestowed on Quinton, but she had at least inherited her beautiful mother's deep violet eyes, and perhaps her fortitude as well.

Augustus Harte sprang to her mind with quick force. She recalled the words that had struck fire in her heart and embarrassment in his. *You, Miss Long, are never but a short step from my heart.* Eyes the golden color of a ripening harvest field had swept over her face and then shyly lowered to study his large, bony hands and wrists that shirt cuffs never quite covered. He'd been a farmer all his life: strong boned, tall, and, to some eyes, gawky. Yet when Adelia had met Augustus, tall and resplendent in his cavalry uniform, he had set her heart racing. She let herself believe that something special had happened between them that night at the small social gathering.

For nearly two years they had corresponded, and then the letters stopped. Every effort to determine where he had gone and what had happened to him ended in failure. Thus she had laid aside any dreams of love and familial happiness. She had been foolish to let herself believe that she was more than a passing interest to Augustus, a faded flower in a field of exotic blooms. What chance did they have, so far apart with letters taking months to arrive—if indeed he had written any letters at all? He had probably married now that the war was over and taken his bride back to Minnesota.

It amazed Adelia as she poured tea into Edward's cup that she could still be affected so deeply by Augustus. She was twenty-five years old and, in most minds of the period, quickly slipping beyond marriageable age. To add insult to injury, there would be no dowry to be given. She'd been assured that the gracious Hiram was willing to marry her despite the family's inability to follow accepted custom. Her fingers trembled on the handle of the teapot. Might love bloom between them later? If not, how could she bear such a life?

She squirmed under the direct gaze of her uncle, wondering if he could discern her thoughts and her longing for Augustus. She was grateful for the absence of Aunt Felicity, whose small, marble-like eyes and puckered lips would reveal her disdain at the foolishness of turning down the well-placed Hiram.

"My dear, the good Lord didn't give us children of our own, and we are of moderate means and in possession of a comfortable home," Edward said. He stretched his neck briefly, as though his collar was too tight. "We are quite prepared to offer you a home with us." Satisfied with his proposal, he leaned his head back against the crocheted antimacassar that protected the fabric from his heavily oiled hair.

Adelia concentrated on setting the teapot down without spilling the hot liquid. Uncle Edward was known for shrewdness, seldom for warmth and affection, and he had a way of turning gifts into obligations. She waited, fearing what was coming next.

"I suppose there's no way we can convince your brother of the folly of heading west, but you will need some means of support now that—" He broke off before referring yet again to the untimely demise of Adelia's father.

She had listened patiently to Quinton's rapt descriptions of the California goldfields. Indeed, the world had been buzzing about it for months ever since President Polk had confirmed that there were "inexhaustible gold mines in California." The president had displayed at the War Department a tea caddy full of gold dust that had arrived from San Francisco as proof. To Congress he announced that there was enough gold in California to pay for the war with Mexico. Newspapers across the country picked up the story, and cities and towns everywhere buzzed with the news. Farmers left their plows, shopkeepers abandoned their businesses, and soldiers even deserted their regiments to head west. "Ho for California!" was the cry everywhere.

Quinton, too, had caught the fever. "Addie, there's so much gold, you can actually pick it up off the ground!" On and on he'd raved about the wagon trains dispatching from places like Independence and St. Joseph, even Kanesville.

"I don't suppose you have been able to dissuade him from such a wanton and irresponsible course," Edward mumbled, drawing his bushy brows together and peering across at his niece.

She said nothing but bit back a retort. It hurt for Quinton to be described in such terms. He wasn't wanton or irresponsible, nor was he stupid. And wasn't it natural for a young, impressionable man to be caught up in the dream of gold just waiting to be harvested?

The incredible discovery near Coloma in January 1848 had seized the imaginations of the world ever since James Marshall found gold in the tailrace of a lumber mill he was building for John Sutter on the American River. Sutter wanted to keep the news quiet, fearing it would ruin his plans for an agricultural empire, but the die was cast.

Rumors spread and were confirmed in March of the same year by a San Francisco newspaper publisher and merchant. Samuel Brannan strode through the streets, holding aloft a vial of gold. "Gold! Gold! Gold from the American River!" he shouted.

Yes, Quinton had caught the fever. Doubtless, there was nothing on earth that would heal him but to head west.

When Adelia said nothing, Edward cleared his raspy throat once more and continued. "As I said, Felicity and I feel responsible for you. Moreover, we have a soft spot in our hearts for my brother's children. We are willing to provide room and board for you. Your brother may head off on a fool's errand, but you will need protection, and it is our duty to do what we can for you. Of course, it would be expected that in return you would provide companionship and serve the needs of Mother Parsons. Due to her grievous headaches, your aunt Felicity has all she can do to keep pace—"

"Oh, forgive me, Uncle!" Adelia leaped up, delighted to hear Quinton's step on the porch. What luck that he had come home at this moment, giving her time to collect her wits and come up with some miracle that would deliver her. *Mother Parsons indeed!* she thought. *A life spent catering to the whims of the cantankerous mother of Aunt Felicity would make an old woman of me in record time.*

Quinton's days at the shop had been grueling. He was still a boy, really, not quite twenty-one. How could one so young look so haggard? Adelia's heart ached for him. She had always guarded him and looked out for his interests from the time he was a toddler. In spite of the five years that separated them, they had been constant companions since childhood. In the weeks since their father died, Quinton had struggled to keep what assets remained of the hardware business he had inherited. But fate had not been kind. The bank had denied a loan, and even the small frame house that provided a roof over their heads was heavily mortgaged.

The slender youth with a cap of curly blond hair hung his coat in the hall and stepped into the parlor. "Uncle Edward." He extended a hand and favored their guest with a smile that didn't quite reach his weary blue eyes. Always aware of his uncle's disdain, Quinton would have been preparing himself for the meeting as soon as he saw the carriage and the matching geldings outside their house.

"Good to see you, my boy." Edward clapped Quinton on the shoulder. "I've just been talking with your dear sister here and extending my condolences."

"That's good of you, Uncle," Quinton said politely. He sat down on the edge of the settle as though poised for flight.

Adelia quickly poured a cup of tea and held it toward him. He looked so tired. His curly hair was wild and unkempt, as though he'd been running his fingers through it. He'd done a lot of that in recent days. The tiny veins in his temples twitched as he cast a wary eye toward Adelia and waited for Uncle Edward to continue.

"You're still intent on pulling up stakes and going to California?"

"It's really the only course I can follow, Uncle," Quinton began patiently. "We have no hope of making it even the rest of this year, and the bank has refused my loan."

"It's a great misfortune indeed." Edward looked away somewhat uncomfortably. Adelia hoped he might loan them what was needed to keep the store and the house, but he had pled financial reverses of his own. Which may or may not be true, Adelia thought uncharitably.

She knew Quinton wasn't bitter over the attitudes of his kin, nor had he asked for aid from them. Perhaps he knew better or his pride wouldn't permit it—and Quinton did have his pride. Young and untested in the ways of the world, he somehow always managed to find a bright spot in the gloom.

"The reports are amazing. A year or so will be enough!" he exclaimed excitedly. "I could bring back plenty of gold to start fresh." He glanced across at Adelia. "We could join one of the trains leaving every day right from Kanesville following the Overland Trail. If we sell the house and store, we'd have enough to outfit a wagon. Why, folks are leaving every day!"

"Have you any idea of the rigors of such a venture?" Edward said. "Imagine traveling across deserts and mountains in a wagon, fighting heat and drought and Indians in search of a pipe dream!"

"Forgive me, Uncle, but it's not a pipe dream," Quinton said, gripping the edge of the settle. He pulled a newssheet from his vest pocket. "It's right here in *The Evening Transcript*: 'By sudden and accidental discovery, the ground is represented to be one vast gold mine. Gold is picked up in pure lumps, twenty-four carats fine . . . In one part of the mine, no other implements are necessary than an ordinary sheath knife to pick the gold from the rocks.'"

"I've read the reports, boy," Edward said with undisguised scorn. "And I haven't missed the ones that tell of men coming back broken in health and spirit, and all for the lure of easy money."

"I know it won't be easy, Uncle," Quinton put in quietly. "But I'm young and strong. I can do this. I know I can. And I want to do it for Addie too."

Edward harrumphed and lifted his round chin. "To the contrary, you need to be a man and persuade your sister that she must not follow along on this foolish course you've set for yourself. I have offered Adelia a proposal to join my family. She's a woman and certainly not up to the kind of deprivation and disaster sure to befall you."

It was all Adelia could do to keep from leaping to her feet. Were women to be forever coddled and clucked over like house pets? Were they to be held back indefinitely from developing their own gifts and skills? She had no quarrel with marriage and family, but couldn't women make other contributions as well?

She stood, planting both feet firmly on the threadbare carpet, and drew herself up to her full five feet six inches. She'd sooner join a convent than live out her days with Edward and Felicity, catering to the whims of Mother Parsons. In the quietest voice she could muster while conveying her firm resolve, she said, "I am most grateful to you and Aunt Felicity, but I am going with Quinton. He will need someone to cook and wash while he's busy at the mines."

Edward got to his feet with some difficulty, his face reddening with the exertion. He opened his mouth but said nothing for several seconds.

Adelia took the opportunity to continue. "Please give my regards to your family, Uncle Edward, and thank you again for your kind offer." She picked up his hat where it lay on the table and handed it to him. "We'll advise you as to the exact plan for departure."

They stood, brother and sister, in polite farewell as their uncle strode to his carriage. When the door closed, Quinton gave a boyish whoop and swung Adelia around and around in his arms.

2

Overland Trail to California
September 1849

"*Y*ou all right, Addie?" Quinton turned around on the wagon seat to peer inside where Adelia sat with her journal, pen poised in a hand that suddenly felt too weak to move.

She eyed her brother fondly. He was tanned as a bronzed statue, his shoulder muscles in permanent flex. Her heart sank with fear and overwhelming pride. A storekeeper was hardly qualified to steer a team of oxen over all-but-impassable mountains and through swollen rivers, but Quinton had kept at it with an endurance she'd never known he possessed. And she would not complain if she could help it. "Fine!" she called with as much cheer as she could muster.

They were crossing the alkali desert, the last forty miles of the trek that had begun in April. Stronger men than Quinton had succumbed to disease or disaster. Some had turned back, their bodies and fortunes spent. "Shall I bring out the canteen?" she called.

Quinton shook his head. His hair beneath his hat was bleached nearly white from sun and dust, and a ragged shirt made into a headband kept the sweat from obscuring his vision as they plodded along. Averaging fifteen to twenty miles a day, they had covered nearly eighteen hundred miles through treacherous and beautiful country. Now, their pace slowed in the searing heat.

Adelia leaned against the bedrolls inside the wagon that had been her home since leaving Iowa. She and Quinton had spent their last seven hundred dollars to outfit the wagon, fitting everything inside its nine-by-five interior. Five hickory hoops that had proved helpful for hanging pots and pans and other necessities held up the roof, made of a cotton fabric waterproofed with linseed oil.

They had packed the wagon with everything *The Emigrants' Guide to Oregon and California* suggested—tools for mining and farming, seeds, medicines, needles and strong thread for mending. They had brought salted bacon and ham, coffee, rice and beans, dried fruits and molasses. In spite of the provisions they had picked up at Fort Laramie and Fort Hall during the six-month-long journey, their food supplies were dwindling fast.

Adelia's body ached from head to foot, but her heart was full. She looked down at the diary in her lap. It was one of few personal possessions that hadn't been lost or thrown out to lighten their load as they trekked across mountain and plain, fording dangerous rivers and treacherous desert. She opened the notebook to the beginning pages that she had filled with sunny description.

> *The plains are covered with flowers. Water and grass abound—more than adequate for our animals and water barrels. Game flourishes everywhere, and Quinton has brought back rabbit and squirrel—even buffalo. In our close-knit, rolling community, everyone pitches in to help. Even the young children have learned to hunt for small game. At night, when we make camp, we share our thoughts and draw strength for the next day's challenges.*

Adelia loved the star-filled nights around the campfire, the stories and songs—even the dancing on nights when they weren't too tired. Always the dream of what lay ahead loomed a shining and powerful portent. She paused, pen in hand, and read on.

I have seldom felt more joyful in my life.

That entry, dated months earlier, charted the first part of their trip. Indeed, she had seldom felt more fulfilled. Long days on the trail had honed her muscles and sharpened her spirit. She even had occasion to drive the oxen to give Quinton a rest or to help out a struggling traveler. But she was most appreciated for her cache of herbs and medicines. An avid student of the human body, she had learned its various ailments and studied potential cures. *If I had been born a man,* she thought, *I might have studied medicine formally.*

Adelia's fingers trembled slightly as she flipped the pages forward.

Chimney Rock, composed of marl and soft sandstone, is shaped like a giant cone, the top rising like a tall tower or chimney. Quint carved our names among the hundreds of others etched into its soft rock.

Scott's Bluff, which their guidebook had deemed "one of the most delightful places that nature ever formed," had made Adelia's spirit soar.

Five miles above the Devil's Gate Canyon, the Sweetwater River cuts through fissures in the rock. The water splashes and roars as though angry to be forced through the narrow openings. The walls on each side rise several hundred feet as though driven in two by some great convulsion of nature.

They had bathed their feet in the rushing waters and tried not to think of the friends they had buried along the way. Cholera was the most dreaded enemy, an enemy none of her herbs or tinctures could heal. Smudged ink on the page was testament to Adelia's tears as she wrote:

> *Emily Holland's husband had to be buried along the trail today. We marked his grave with a small wooden cross Jemima Smith found in her sewing basket.*

A few had turned back under the daunting rigors of the trail, but most of the emigrants had persevered. Many looked rail thin and years older than when the trip began, but their hopes remained steadfast. Adelia looked down at her hands, rough and chapped, the nails broken and stained. She knew her hair was bleached and dry from dust and sun, her skin red and parched in spite of the coconut oil she daubed on it nightly. *If Augustus were to see me now,* she ruminated.

At night, when the campfire flickered and her heart yearned for home, his face would intrude. And she would remember the words that had struck fire in her heart: *You, Miss Long, are never but a short step from my heart.* He was clever with words and would smile shyly over his puns about his name and "long" and "short." Why couldn't she stop thinking of him?

She closed her diary and picked her way forward to crouch next to Quinton. "Let me take over for a while. You need to rest." She handed him the canteen he had insisted he didn't need.

He glanced at her with eyes red from dust and strain. "No need, Sis," he said through parched lips. "Hoke will be wanting a break from that ornery mule of his. He'll take the reins for a while."

As though he'd been summoned, Henry "Hoke" Adams, grizzled and gray as the mule he rode, drew up alongside their wagon. "Afternoon," he called, tipping the brim of his colorless sombrero. "And to you, little missy," he added in a creaky voice several tones higher than when they'd first met. Parched throats and tongues could bedevil speech, and it was a shame to silence the unflappable old mountain man whose wit and cunning had not only entertained them around campfires but had also saved them from more than one disaster on the trail.

Hoke had joined the company at Fort Laramie along with several other men who chose to travel by horse or mule. They packed their supplies in enormous saddlebags, making their mounts appear hugely pregnant as they wobbled from side to side. Tools and guns hung from every available appendage of their tackle, even pots and pans. Hoke was probably not more than fifty-five, but that was old along the Overland Trail. He bore life with surprising zest and indomitable goodwill.

Even the proud Wylie Hunter, self-appointed leader of the pack, grudgingly listened to Hoke's advice. The broad-shouldered, handsome, but unrelenting Mr. Hunter had goaded them on through drought and rain, keeping a kind of patched-together order and chiding anyone who slackened the pace. He'd been in charge of his regiment in the Mexican-American War, and the emigrants recognized his experience, even if they didn't always appreciate his methods.

"A thousand more are headed for the fields," he would warn. "I'm not letting them get there ahead of us. Now, step it up, you men! Ho for California!" Switching off between two enormous horses, he would trot up and down the line of wagons, giving orders, checking on any wagon that stalled, and, by sheer force of will, drove the beleaguered company toward the Sierra Nevada Mountains. Was he driven by greed? *Perhaps*, Adelia thought. *But would we have made it this far without the unyielding Wylie Hunter?*

"It's hot enough to fry your taters in midair!" Hoke said, hoisting himself up onto the wagon seat. "Best be rationing that water unless you've a mind to fry along with them taters before we get to the diggings."

Adelia smiled as her brother joined her inside to rest against the rolls of bedding they had managed to salvage from the Humboldt River. At that swollen crossing, the men were forced to wade back and forth in water to their shoulders, drawing emptied wagons to a midpoint where men on the opposite bank waded out to connect chains hitched to oxen onshore. Goods were taken across in a skiff and cattle prodded into swimming.

Thank God for Hoke, Adelia thought. The cunning mountain man seemed to possess the strength of ten men. Now, as he urged the oxen forward, she pressed a cloth with a bit of precious water to Quinton's mottled face. Wind and sun had burned his skin and etched crevices into its youthful layers. They had been traveling through the night, Hunter pushing them to make the foot of the Sierras by daylight. But daylight was long past, and the desert stretched on. "Just rest awhile," she whispered tenderly to her brother. But Quinton was already asleep, arms and legs flung out in hapless abandon.

"What will become of us?" she whispered, knowing he could not hear her. They had set off with such excitement and unrestrained joy. *And persevered*, she reminded herself. Even through Quinton's still face and closed eyelids she read an unquenchable hope. She would remain strong for him. *And for myself*, she added quietly as lines from a hymn sang themselves to her. *When other helpers fail, and comforts flee, Help of the helpless, O abide with me!*

Hearing the fast *clip-clop* of a horse, she peered through the flap of the wagon. Hunter, tall in the saddle of a mottled, once-black horse, headed toward their wagon. A bandana to ward off sun and dust covered his face beneath smoldering dark eyes.

Black hair flared beneath his wide slouch hat. He leaned forward in the saddle, pressing the toes of his boots into the horse's sides, and stopped alongside. Adelia scooted out to join Hoke on the wooden seat, careful not to wake Quinton.

Hunter yanked his bandana down to reveal a generous nose and prominent chin covered with a black beard. Chiseled lips relaxed to a degree just short of a smile as he drew up and gave her a brief nod. He looked every inch a military officer, handsome despite the harshness of the desert. His commanding eyes roved over her face and hair.

Adelia looked down, unnerved by his piercing eyes and embarrassed about her shabby clothes and tangled hair. There were times on the trail when Hunter's manner of looking at her made her more than a little uneasy. Or was it just that she was the only single woman on the train? Still, her traveling companions had treated her with the utmost respect.

"We're in need of your assistance, Miss Long," he said, his voice surprisingly strong, given the amount of dust and debris that cloaked the atmosphere. "The lady in the Kramer wagon is sick. See what you can do for her. I'll take you back, but mind you, we can't afford any delays." He slapped the rear edge of his saddle to indicate that she should mount behind him.

She hesitated, then reached for her tapestry bag in which she kept her herbs and medicines. She had learned their use when called upon to care for neighbors back in Iowa. The Kramer wagon was at the end of the line, having dropped back more than a few times due to various issues, often because of ailing children. Now the mother was apparently in need. "Can we not stop briefly to give them a rest?" Adelia asked.

"No time. We've got to keep moving. We lost enough time at the Sink. There's a hundred at our heels. I didn't take this trip to find nothing but mud and rocks at the end of the trail!"

He was holding out an arm for Adelia to mount behind him. She was pressed against his body and forced to grab hold around his chest as he sped to the back of the train. The heat generated through his sweaty shirt made her slightly breathless. It had been a long time since she was that close to any man. Relief mingled with regret when Hunter slowed to come into pace and eased her onto the wagon.

Orpah Kramer lay amidst grimy blankets, surrounded by two of her four children. The older two walked alongside the wagon, their faces drawn, casting piteous looks inside. Adelia gave them each a quarter stick of precious sugar cane. "Go along now. I will see to your mother," she said gently, shooing them away from the sound of their mother's coughs and moans.

Adelia lifted the consumptive woman's head and pressed a few drops of water between her parched lips. She could feel the heat radiating from her without testing for fever. Drenching rains, merciless heat, and the rigor of bumping along in a wagon over rocky ground had taken its toll on her delicate frame. Adelia pulled a handkerchief from her apron pocket and poured a generous amount of water in it. She touched the cloth to Orpah's hot face and arms. "There, now," she whispered as she might to a frightened child. "It will be all right."

Adelia drew in her breath. If only she were a real doctor. Many had succumbed to disease since they'd left Iowa, and the only doctor on the train had turned back when his wife became too ill to travel. She would do what she could, but would it really be all right? She whispered a prayer loud enough for Orpah to hear, hoping she would be comforted by the familiar words.

At their last encampment, she had mixed a tincture of horse-radish root and saturated her last two pieces of flannel with the plaster. *An ounce of preparation—if not prevention—is worth a pound of cure,* she had thought then. Now she needed the herb, well known for its antibacterial and expectorant properties. Gently, she placed one on the sick woman's chest to help relieve congestion and administered laudanum to lessen the pain. The rest would be up to the Almighty and to Orpah's constitution.

She collected the soiled laundry strewn about the patient's makeshift bed and collected bits of crockery and tin. There was no food, spoiled or otherwise, and likely hadn't been for the last several miles. She handed a large dried plum to each of the toddlers and read a portion of Scripture from the battered Bible she found in the mess of blankets. Gradually, the woman's labored breathing became easier, the hacking coughs fewer in number. Perhaps she could return to her own wagon now. She considered covering the ground on foot when she heard hoofbeats and the weak whinny of a tired horse.

"Ho in the Kramer cabin!" came Hunter's strident voice.

Adelia scrambled to the back of the wagon as the sick woman stirred and groaned. She pulled aside the flap. "Hush!" she demanded. "She's finally resting." She cast him a harsh glance and hopped down, careful not to catch her long skirt in the rolling wheel.

He scowled at the rebuke but said nothing as he reached down to lift her up. They trotted along slowly, moving steadily up to the front. Adelia and Quinton's wagon was second in the queue, a position they'd held almost since the beginning. The extreme heat of the day was passing. If all went well, they'd reach the diggings by dusk.

Hope swelled in her heart. They were going to make it! Soon, they would be raking up the precious gold that would change their fortunes forever. They could return with their heads held high. That would show Uncle Edward and the condescending Hiram Powell. They would return with enough money to buy a new hardware store and make their father proud. Could he see them from the great beyond? Was he cheering them on? Adelia allowed her heart these bolstering thoughts, though her mind argued for caution.

Suddenly, Wylie pulled up short, and every muscle in his back went rigid. Adelia peered around him, noticing at the same time that the wagons had slowed almost to a stop.

"What in tarnation?" Wylie exclaimed under his breath.

Adelia's heart thudded, and she felt herself grow cold. A band of Indians, bronzed bodies gleaming, blocked the passage of the train. Their chests were bare but for a blanket over one shoulder and a strap girding their loins. Some were stalled on horseback, faces fierce in the blazing sun. Others stood alongside their steeds with sharp, pointed sticks in their hands.

"Diggers!" Wylie said through gritted teeth.

The guidebook had warned of the native people of the region, a tribe known as Diggers because of their custom of digging edible roots and insects. They lived off these in the harsh desert, and the women stored food for the winter in mounds. It was rumored that the Diggers raided white campgrounds at night, stole their food and animals, and poisoned their water. Adelia had read about the massacres of harmless white men, how Indians had tortured women and carried away innocent babies. Were they to become casualties just as their journey was about to end?

Wylie started advancing toward them slowly, his hand moving to the revolver on his left hip.

"Wait!" she whispered fiercely in his ear. "Maybe we can appease them." They had encountered Indians before—the Pawnee earlier in their journey with whom they had traded molasses and jewelry for buffalo meat. Adelia grasped the handles of her tapestry bag and jumped down from Wylie's great black horse.

She walked toward the formidable group, opening her bag. As she passed the wagons, making her way to Hoke and Quinton, she pulled out a long string of buttons and waved the colorful stream high like a flag of surrender. Silence was palpable, the men on high alert, women and children huddled inside their wagons.

"Please, don't let them go for their rifles," she prayed. "Please, let these be peaceful Indians who will not harm us." Her heart hammered in her chest. It must not be over now, just a few miles short of the treasured goldfields.

3

Cabot Falls, Vermont
Present Day

"What do you think?" The man stepped back from his canvas and extended a hand daubed with yellow paint.

Sofia Parker surveyed the artist's canvas, a sea of disjointed shapes in yellow and black. Streaks of red passed through like shards of glass.

"I call it *Dusk to Dawn*," he announced proudly, lifting his chin with its graying beard neatly trimmed to a point. "It represents the sun breaking through the night blackness. The sun is ultimately victorious, but first, there's a bloody struggle."

Sofia resisted the urge to laugh. Ernest Haynes was a new student, one of two she'd agreed to teach on Saturdays to accommodate his work schedule and her own need to bring in some extra cash. Avid if meagerly talented, Haynes had chosen to take classes with her, though he had the wherewithal to study with more-prestigious artists. His family, so it was said, was quite well connected in Boston. In Cabot Falls, Ernest's money, not to mention his braggadocio, was becoming legendary. Family pride seemed to be his dominant characteristic.

When Sofia's husband, Jim, had questioned her decision to interrupt her Saturdays with art lessons, she had been careful not to name money as the reason. A man like Jim, who worked harder than most and provided well for his family, shouldn't be made to feel inadequate. He hadn't yet regained his usual vigor after a bad bout of the flu. Anxious to keep her money worries from him, she had insisted that taking on the extra art classes was something she wanted to do as an artist. After all, it was often the teacher who became the learner.

The truth was they were feeling the pinch of extra expenses. They'd had to buy a new furnace, property taxes had risen dramatically, and recent repairs to her car rivaled the national debt, at least to someone trying to balance the family budget. The extra art classes could ease things a little, along with the small contract she had taken to provide cakes for a bakery expanding its business.

"So, may I have your expert opinion, Mrs. Parker?" Ernest urged, interrupting her reverie somewhat coldly. His eyes narrowed in his florid face as he viewed his masterpiece with something akin to adoration.

Sofia took a deep breath, nodding to show she was giving his work careful study. Ernest was a bachelor who handled his wealthy father's investment interests in Cabot Falls where he had recently settled. Though he claimed that the "small, provincial town" was appealing enough, he made it known that he, the consummate cosmopolitan, aspired to be the next Picasso.

"It certainly does depict struggle," she ventured, "and the contrast is good." She cocked her head, trying to make sense of the thing while weighing her words. "The red streaks, though, may be a bit overdone. You might want to soften them a little."

"But that's the genius of it!" Ernest said, his dainty beard seeming to wiggle in protest. "The strong crimson color makes the whole painting."

Muttering something about balance and form, she hoped to deflect his quick offense. She had learned from the start that Ernest Haynes Jr. wouldn't be the easiest student.

Suddenly, she was aware that Marjorie Bennett, her other

Saturday student, had left her easel and was peering at Ernest's painting. In her late sixties, Marjorie worked in a small boutique that sold expensive designer dresses and overpriced baubles. She wore her gray hair in a loose bun from which tendrils of silver hair danced in thin swirls. A black velvet ribbon tied around her thin neck with a cameo attached gave her a comical Gibson Girl effect, which was all the more odd, given her age.

"Well, I think it's all right if you like chaos," Marjorie quipped. She was not known for diplomacy but was somewhat renowned as a local gossip. Her snappish brown eyes narrowed in her heavily powdered face with its two bright spots of rouge. "Everyone knows that real art should speak of beauty and order."

"Not necessarily," Sofia ventured, feeling her temples pulsate. If Ernest aspired to be the next Picasso, Marjorie Bennett saw herself as the reincarnation of Georgia O'Keefe.

Ernest jerked a thumb toward Marjorie's easel. "I suppose those blobs of garish color you've spattered on the canvas speak of something," he muttered, drawing himself up to his full five feet eight inches. "Kindergarten! That's what it says to me."

Good heavens. These two are worse than children. Sofia gave them both her speech on "helpful" criticism and art as individual expression and ordered them back to their stations. She felt like a referee at a boxing match.

Seventeen-year-old Vanessa stuck her head inside the room. "Mom, I need—" she began.

Frowning, Sofia excused herself and went to Vanessa, partially closing the door to the adjoining four-season room where she taught. The room overlooked the beautifully landscaped back lawn and woods and provided inspiration for the creative spirit.

"Sorry to interrupt," Vanessa said sheepishly. Like the rest of Sofia and Jim's children, she honored the privacy of the four-season room when Mom was working.

"It's all right." Sofia rolled her eyes. "Actually, this time you may have saved my sanity."

"Mom, I really need to borrow some money so I can go horseback riding with Jen and Sue this afternoon. I'm short about twenty dollars."

"*I need!*" *The perennial child's cry.* Sofia sighed. *When did children learn the difference between "need" and "want"?* She went into the kitchen and drew a mug from the cupboard. She hated to deny Vanessa, who was really quite good with her money and often took on babysitting jobs to buy the things she wanted. She was anything but lazy. But horseback riding cost a fortune. Sofia drew in her breath.

Luke, noisily crunching his breakfast cereal, piped up. "Yeah, and I'm gonna need ten bucks for some dumb textbook on Monday."

"Textbooks aren't dumb," she said firmly. "And why did you wait till the last minute to tell me?" Sofia sat down at the kitchen table next to Wynter, her fifteen-year-old, who looked dazed as she stared at the cereal box. Any time short of noon was too early to get up on a Saturday as far as Wynter was concerned. Perhaps she wasn't awake enough to chime in with her "needs." Looking at her, Sofia couldn't help thinking of the audiologist's bill that needed to be paid.

Ten-year-old Matthew, who'd eaten breakfast at seven, came bounding in, a tiny collector car in each hand, which he clanked together noisily. "Can I have two dollars for that jet plane I showed you? It's the coolest." He had obviously moved on from cars to air transportation.

"Look, kids," she said quietly, putting her mug down firmly. "You're forgetting what we talked about last week. It's really important that we stretch our money for a little while. As we discussed, you're going to have to make do with your allowances and not ask for anything extra. Not from your dad either." She gave them a severe look to underscore her meaning.

She toyed with imaginary crumbs on the vinyl tablecloth. The kids had been taught to save for the things they wanted, and they really didn't ask for much. But money was really tight. *How do you make kids understand? It's so hard to deny them when you want to give them the world.*

Vanessa swallowed, obviously recalling their important talk before her father came home for supper the night before. "I know," she said glumly. She quickly brightened, her quick brown eyes fervent. She took her job as the eldest and therefore the most responsible seriously. "It's okay. I can go riding next weekend instead."

Luke pushed back his cereal bowl and shrugged. "Who needs another textbook anyway?"

"School is different. You'll get your textbook, young man," Sofia said.

"Does that mean I don't get my plane?" Matthew queried, grabbing an apple from the green bowl as consolation.

Wynter broke in. "You got that right, genius!" she told him. "Besides, remember the garage sale plan we came up with yesterday? Have you gone through that junk in your room and found something we can sell?"

Matthew shrugged again. "I'm working on it."

Last week, while Jim was away at a teachers' meeting, Sofia and the children had gone through the basement storage area and identified expendable items for the sale. It was the children's idea, and she was delighted with their plan. They wouldn't get rich, but the sale would bring in a few dollars. Besides, they might get rid of some of the clutter that had been collecting down there.

"Why don't we bring up the boxes we've already marked for the sale and work on pricing?" Vanessa suggested. "It looks kind of cloudy and nasty today anyway." Vanessa was fully engaged now. "Matthew and Luke can carry the boxes up. Wynter and I will get tags and markers."

"Why not?" Sofia agreed. "But just bring up only one or two boxes. We'll start pricing here on the kitchen table. That way, I can keep my eye on Marjorie and Mr. Haynes in case they need me—if they ever stop bickering and get back to work, that is. We have to keep a path clear for their trips to the kitchen for coffee. Not to mention bathroom stops." Marjorie either had the weakest bladder in history or she enjoyed snooping in her hostess's house. But Sofia wanted her students to feel comfortable and free to come and go. She swept Matthew's brown thatch of hair off his forehead. "Put your dishes in the sink, and go give your muscles a workout."

Sofia stepped into the four-season room, glad to see her two students busy at their assignments, though the atmosphere of artistic antagonism in the room might well be cut with a knife. She was gratified to see that Ernest had painted over some of the red slashes, which sadly did little to enhance his masterpiece. She encouraged him and the aspiring Georgia O'Keefe until she heard the thump on the table, signaling that the boys had located the boxes.

She went back into the kitchen. "You got the ones marked with a G, right?"

"Yup," Luke said, pointing to the letter marked on the top of a large box. "G for garage sale."

Matthew appeared seconds later with a midsize box. No G in sight. "Where'd you get that one?" she asked as Matthew panted heavily, most likely for her benefit. "Never mind. We'll see if there's anything in it we can use."

As the general hubbub continued, Matthew pushed the smaller, unmarked box toward Sofia. She carefully removed the brown tape and opened the flaps. Material of a deep crimson lay folded inside—the Italian drapes that had hung in her grandmother's house for as long as she could remember. Nonna had given them to her, but, knowing they were much too formal for their house, Sofia had never even taken them from the box.

She touched the carefully folded fabric. Remembering Nonna was a bittersweet affair. Sofia would probably never stop missing her grandmother, Elena Baresi. But she would always be grateful for the way she made her feel—worthy and strong, qualities she still wasn't sure she had the right to claim.

She unfolded the first drape, which was threadbare and faded from years of sun. The boys, quickly losing interest, went scrounging in the refrigerator. Vanessa looked on respectfully, and Wynter turned her nose up at the contents. "They smell moldy. Fifty cents maybe?"

When Sofia unfolded the second drape, something fell out onto the floor. Luke picked up a worn leather pouch about the size of the bag that held his marble collection. "Hey, how'd that get in there?" But opening the pouch, he screwed up his face.

Sofia lifted the sack from his hands, felt the softness of old leather. A tag was attached to the leather thong that held the pouch closed. She loosened the string carefully and looked inside.

"It looks like gold," Vanessa said, peering over Sofia's shoulder. "What's the tag say?"

A kind of hush fell over everyone in the kitchen as Sofia studied the faded and somewhat blurry writing. "'It made fools of us all,'" she read thoughtfully.

"A bag of gold!" Matthew shouted, knocking the napkin holder off the table in his eagerness to get a closer look. "But it could be fool's gold like that stuff down by the creek. It's called mica," he said importantly.

"That's pyrite, not mica," Wynter observed sagely. "There's a number and some letters on the tag," she said, then drew back. "Yuck! Gross!"

Sofia squinted. The letters appeared to be *V. N.*, but they were so faint and marred, it was difficult to be sure. One of the two visible numbers looked like a seven or a two. Could they have something to do with the quilt that Nonna had willed to her? Each block in the heirloom was numbered to accord with entries in the diary.

She couldn't have been more surprised when she learned the quilt and diary were to be hers. Her sisters, Rosa and Gina, were the quilters, the talented needlewomen. The obvious choices, they were as surprised as Sofia over their grandmother's bequest.

"Wasn't there something in the diary about gold? About that lady who went west with her brother?" Vanessa offered.

Sofia searched her memory. There *had* been something like that in the diary, but there was much she'd only glossed over. So many lives and adventures were clustered in its pages.

But where did the bag come from? Why had Nonna kept it? Or had it accidentally fallen into the box when she packed up her old drapes? Luke was probably right that the stuff in the bag was fool's gold, and yet, maybe . . . She shook her head, aware that her curiosity and penchant for riddle solving had begun to rise to the surface.

"Go get the diary, Vanessa. You know where I keep the key."

She was back in a flash, carrying the precious document, and Sofia scanned the pages until she found a letter with the headline *Mok Hill, California*. She began reading, the children clustering around her: *Quinton's claim is yielding a good amount of gold. We are both full of gratitude for this success. Mr. Hunter tells us there is much yet to be coaxed from the rocks and riverbeds.* Could it be that this was an actual sampling of that treasure? Sofia stared at the lines penned in narrow script and felt her excitement rise.

The children were talking at once about what they could do with a whole bag of gold. Wynter began prancing about runway-style as though she were a model in an elegant gown. Luke was sure Great-Grandma had been captured by pirates and began posturing around the kitchen, whooping about treasure chests. In the midst of the commotion, Sofia looked up to see Ernest and Marjorie watching from the doorway, their artists' easels abandoned.

"Oh!" Sofia exclaimed, closing the diary and pushing the leather bag back into the box. *How long have they been standing there?* With the toe of her shoe, she shoved the box under the table and turned to Marjorie and Ernest. "Sorry for all the noise. We were just going through some stuff for a garage sale."

"Yeah, and Mom found a whole bag of gold from Muck Hill! We're gonna be rich," Matthew sang. "It's all in the diary our great-grandma left."

"Mok Hill," Luke put in knowingly, correcting his brother. "The gold came from some place called Mok Hill in California." Then echoing Matthew's earlier commentary, he added, "But I bet it's nothing but pyrite."

"Mr. Featherbrain knows all," Wynter mocked, rolling her eyes.

"That's enough foolishness," Sofia said, raising her voice. She passed the diary in an underhand motion to Vanessa, who stood behind her. "Put it away," she said in a low voice, then stood, making shooing motions to the children. "You have homework to do," she said severely. "Now out, all of you." Sofia turned to her wide-eyed students. "I don't mean you," she said, embarrassed.

The children quickly disappeared, leaving a scowling Ernest with an expression she couldn't name. Marjorie looked like she'd just swallowed the most delicious secret in the world.

Ernest harrumphed in wounded pride. "Didn't mean to pry," he muttered, but his big eyes flashed from Sofia's face to Vanessa's disappearing form.

"I'm sorry for all this confusion," Sofia began, feeling her face grow hot with embarrassment. "It's really nothing." When neither of her students budged, she added meaningfully, "I'll be back with you in a minute."

Ernest's dark brows furrowed in his florid face. After a second or two, he headed back into the four-season room, looking somewhat startled or confused. *All the commotion probably offended his artistic sensibilities,* Sofia thought uncharitably. She was still more than a little miffed at the man's arrogant behavior.

"And I was just going to the little girls' room," Marjorie said, lifting her nose in the air.

Little girls' room. Marjorie hasn't been a little girl for more than half a century. Sofia clamped her mouth shut.

"When I heard you'd found gold, I just had to see for myself," Marjorie said.

Oh, great. Miss Nosey will blow things out of all proportion. The mere mention of gold—even fool's gold—does strange things to people. Even when it is all a tempest in a teapot.

"Never mind, dear," Marjorie said sweetly, crossing her knobby hands over the cameo at her throat. "Your secret's safe with me."

Sofia had hardly drawn a settling breath when she heard a knock at the back door. The serviceman from Harvey's Heating and Cooling was there to do the quarterly contracted furnace check. Sofia groaned. Payment would be expected when he was finished. She ushered Marjorie back to the four-season room and returned to admit a serviceman she didn't recall seeing before. Dark-skinned with a mop of straight black hair, he stood patiently on the porch, looking in the window through a pair of very dark eyes. How long had he been standing there?

Sofia pointed the way to the basement and went up to her bedroom to find her checkbook. She couldn't help dropping down in exhaustion on her bed. Five minutes—that's all she dared allow herself. Her students would be waiting, and if she was lucky, they'd have her fee ready, all of which and more would go to cover the furnace maintenance.

If it weren't so disconcerting, it might be funny. Taunting her with a silly story about gold just when money was in short supply. A joke Nonna was playing in absentia? But Nonna wasn't like that. Maybe the truth about the dusty old bag would come out when she had time to really study the diary.

That time was not now, nor would it be any time soon. Tomorrow was Sunday. Besides church, there was a wedding in the afternoon, and she'd promised the kids tacos and an evening of backyard Baggo. On Monday morning, she would get up at the crack of dawn to begin baking. She had agreed to provide eight dozen cupcakes and a triple batch of coconut macaroons for Heather Cookson's fledgling business. Why, oh why had she agreed to that? Especially on the night Rosa and Gina were coming for dinner. They'd expect her usual Italian specialties.

Cherish the day. Embrace the adventure. She could still hear Nonna's voice.

Life was an adventure, all right, but at the moment, a deserted island in the Pacific sounded really good to Sofia.

4

Overland Trail
September 1849

Adelia's heart thumped wildly as she and Wylie Hunter approached the band of scantily clad Indians. Hunter clutched the gun strapped to his hip. "Diggers," he muttered under his breath.

"Wait, let me talk to them," she whispered desperately.

"If they don't kill us, they'll steal us blind and bury the stash in the ground like blasted desert rats!" he said.

But Hoke, who'd had run-ins with them in the past, had once told her they had a powerful reason to mistrust the white man. "Digger squaws, when threatened by white invaders, would bury their children in the sand," Hoke had said. "They'd warn them young'uns not to make a sound until the owl-faced men were gone.

"Chief Winnemucca's granddaughter once stayed buried all day long, listening to lizards, mice, and scorpions scuttlin' through the sand," he told them as they had gathered around a campfire. "Her mother finally rescued her, but the owl-faced men done burned the grass and mud mounds where they stored their food for winter. Ain't no wonder they feel put out." He had pulled meditatively on his scraggly beard. "It's enough to make a body spit fire."

Now, as she looked at the threatening scene ahead, Adelia felt her stomach roll. Atrocities had been perpetrated on both sides out of fear or greed. As they advanced along the line of wagons, there was no sound, save the stamping and breathing of exhausted horses and oxen. Adelia swallowed hard, her knees knocking. They were within sight of their destination.

Is it all to end here?

She moved forward steadily, keeping her head level. Their wagon was stalled along the ridge where the group of Indians stood. Hoke's presence just might increase their chances for a peaceful resolution. If one were possible. What were these painted men thinking as they stood with spears in their hands, their faces dark with sun and dirt?

Adelia advanced, giving their visitors what she hoped was a friendly smile. Perhaps she wasn't beautiful, but she was young and strong and possessed of feminine virtues. They were staring at her, at her hair, bleached platinum by the sun, and her sweeping calico skirt rustling softly as she moved. Women were a rarity along the trail. Sometimes they were treasured for that uniqueness. Sometimes they were stolen for the same quality. She felt herself shiver in the heat.

Most of the Indians were old and gray-headed. Feathers drooped from thin bands tied at their wrinkled foreheads. Standing apart and half-hidden by a scrub bush, a young brave stood watching, bare brown arms hanging soldierlike at his sides. He was rail thin and sinewy, with black hair that hung loose from a raglike band circling his forehead. Deep-set eyes bored from their hollowed-out cavities. A scowl pulled his sculpted lips down. He looked wary and threatening, yet at the same time inquisitive, even longing. Adelia felt a strange wave of sympathy mitigating her fear.

She stopped near the wagon where Quinton and Hoke waited in silence. Behind them, no one moved in the halted caravan. She smiled more widely as she drew up to the fierce-looking group of bronzed men and held out the buttons. At the South Pass, they'd traded flashy trinkets for dried buffalo meat when they had been accosted by a similar group. These Indians, too, might be inclined to a swap, though she saw nothing edible that they might offer in trade. They all looked as though they needed a good meal themselves.

"For you," she said, proffering the shiny buttons. "Please take them."

Hoke's craggy voice drifted down warily from his perch. "They can't eat buttons, Addie. Here," he said, holding out a bag of corn flour. From another wagon, a loaf of bread appeared at the end of an outstretched arm, a jar of molasses from another farther down the line. She collected them and placed them on the ground near the Indians' feet.

As she straightened, the oldest and most decorated man—the chief perhaps—turned toward the youth and gave a stern, guttural command. The young brave hesitated briefly, then stepped out from the camouflage. Favoring his right leg, he limped toward the gifts on the ground and scrambled to retrieve them. He dropped them into the outstretched hands of two braves standing next to the old man, adorned with a heavily feathered headdress. Then he scrabbled backward, a drudge doing his master's bidding, and returned to his station behind a rock.

The brave's compelling eyes continued to bore into hers, not with malice but with a kind of silent appeal. Adelia stared back. Who was he, and why was he being treated like a servant or some kind of outcast? How had he been injured?

The old chief made a swift, cutting motion and jerked his face up. The band of Indians dispersed soundlessly, the expressions on their dark faces impassive. Only the crippled brave stood still, watching. The sun glanced off something silver attached to a scary-looking necklace of claws that hung around his neck. Then he, too, disappeared from sight.

We've been spared by the Lord's good providence, Adelia penned in her journal when they were once again underway, the wagons creaking and groaning over the last few miles to the foot of the magnificent Sierras. *We are nearly at the goldfields. What awaits us there I cannot imagine, but we will work and trust the outcome to God.*

They had discussed where to set up their camp, paying particular attention to the advice of Wylie Hunter, who had more knowledge of the area than anyone else. Often, around the campfire, they had begged Wylie to tell them about the diggings.

Once Hannibal Reed, a grim-faced farmer from Indiana, asked, "Do we have a chance?"

Wiley's jaw had twitched in the firelight. "It's filling up fast," he had said grimly. "There's gold being washed out of the Sierras for three hundred miles, but the good places will soon all be taken. Why do you think I've been pushing so hard to get to the gold before the vultures make off with it?"

Then he had turned on his heel and strode into the woods as though he were being chased.

Vultures? Adelia wondered. *Are we vultures too? What sets us apart from them? Are we not all seeking gold to get back to our homes and families as soon as we can? To make a fresh start?* Surely, there was enough for everyone.

But Wylie seemed unwilling to give quarter to any man. She had stared after his departing form, unnerved by his apparent lust for gold.

Their plan was to camp along one of several rivers that emptied into the San Joaquin. Men were hard at work lining the Cosumnes, Calaveras, and Stanislaus as the sun beamed down upon them. Along the Mokelumne River, the terrain turned softer, gentler, and more rolling. Wylie parsed the area with shrewd eyes and declared that the promise of gold along its banks was rumored to be strong. The Mokelumne it was, with Hunter as their continued guide.

In spite of his extreme weariness, Quinton took no time to rest from the rigorous journey. His sunburned face had become gaunt and stubbly, and the cough he'd told Adelia repeatedly not to worry about seemed deeper, more worrisome. Adelia watched Quinton and Hoke trudge off toward the river with their tools and the wooden rocker box they had made over long hours on the trail.

Hoke praised the virtues of the "cradle" over the pan. It was a combination washing box and screen with a canvas apron under it, a short sluice with two riffles and rockers under it. The bottom of the washing box was made of sheet metal with holes a half inch in diameter punched through it. The bottom of the rocker was made of a single wide, smooth board.

Adelia smiled, thankful for the light that burned in her brother's eyes. Tales of abundant goldfields had instilled new life and confidence in him, and meeting Hoke on the trail had clinched his resolve.

Hoke, however, didn't mince any words about the rigors of life on the goldfields. "Standing in freezing rivers and coaxing ore from ground as hard as steel ain't easy," he said. "Purely backbreaking, that's what it is! But when you bring up that pan and she fairly glitters with gold, it's enough to make a hog spit in a rabbit's eye!"

Everyone laughed at Hoke's colorful speech rendered with his mountain twang, Quinton most of all. He had come to depend on Hoke. Over the long months on the trail, he had begun to look up to him as something of a father figure. And Hoke had taken to Quinton. It might have had something to do with the way Quinton had spoken up for him when Wylie Hunter had dismissed him as a "washed-up old prospector."

"Addie and I would be pleased to have you set up camp with us," Quinton had said while on the trail nearing the Sierras. He had rubbed his blistered hands nervously, eager eyes hopeful.

"I'm used to going it alone—me and old Ruby there," Hoke had replied, nodding toward the pack mule trudging along beside the wagon. But there was a gleam in his old eyes that said he was pleased. "Truth to tell, though, going it alone ain't amounted to much." He paused, still rubbing a chapped hand over his scraggly beard. "I'll cogitate on it."

He didn't cogitate long. Hoke and Quinton agreed to mine together on adjoining claims. They shook on it before they reached the Mokelumne.

The camp was composed of several tents, a log-fenced corral for animals, and a couple of patched-together shacks. There was plenty of space in their fledgling new community, at least for now. Residents had enough land to set up their individual tents, yet they were close enough to come to one another's aid should the need arise.

They anchored the wagon that would serve as Adelia's home on a ridge a mile and a half from the riverbank and set up two tents—one for Quinton to sleep in and one to hold Adelia's cook-stove and supplies. Hoke, though partnering with Quinton, pitched his tent farther upriver. More gold seekers would be heading for the fields, following the fabled California riverbeds in search of gold, but Adelia enjoyed a measure of privacy beneath the spreading cottonwoods.

The sound of their hammers and pickaxes carried on the wind as miners built rude lean-tos for shelter. Quinton promised to build a cabin before winter when the cold rains would set in, but for now, mild temperatures and blue skies reigned. Adelia thanked God for their safety and the promise of gold to fulfill their needs. She should be too busy to be lonely, but sometimes the silence lay heavy in the middle of the day when the men were away. She longed for feminine company.

Charity Reed had joined their camp, along with her husband, Hannibal, and her son, a sallow-faced child of ten whom Adelia had treated for dysentery during the long journey. Hannibal had stammered his thanks after Adelia sat through a long night on the trail with the fever-ridden boy. Charity hardly even asked after the boy. To be fair, she had been ill herself and most days lay on a dingy mattress, tossing her head of stringy black hair and muttering under her breath.

Charity had once been a singer in variety shows back East, or so the talk went. The popular form of American stage entertainment was first conceived as saloon shows. Circus acts, singers, dancers, chorus girls, and bawdy comics were presented in whatever proportion each manager preferred. Any abandoned church, barn, or warehouse could be converted for variety use. The resulting spaces were often shabby but almost always profitable. Owners called them "palaces," "museums," "free and easies," and "wine halls." By any name, they were still saloons.

How she had come to leave the stage and marry Hannibal Reed was anyone's guess, but it was rumored that Hannibal and the boy tented together close to the diggings while Charity slept alone in the wagon. It was said that she mourned the loss of a second child, a baby girl who died of cholera before they left Indiana.

"You won't get any thanks for your trouble," Constance White had said when Adelia went to tend the ailing boy while still on the Overland Trail. "I brought her a pot of lentil soup, seeing she had nothing in her wagon, but she just turned her face away. She ain't got a kind word for any of us—no word at all." Constance, a stout woman of forty-eight, had come west with her husband and settled along the Calaveras. *Constance would have been good company,* Adelia thought sadly. But Charity seemed without a modicum of the quality her name suggested. Or had sorrow robbed her of grace and goodness?

On the second day after their arrival, Adelia found herself uncommonly weary after preparing lunch and taking it to Quinton and Hoke at the diggings. There was much to be done, but she must guard her health for all their sakes. She settled back against the pillow inside her wagon, drowsy and oddly at peace. She felt a strange sense of being watched over, as though she were a child again with her mother at her bedside, smoothing her forehead. With sweet weariness, she allowed herself the luxury of sleep.

When she woke, the sun was slowly sliding westward. Her brother and Hoke would be returning when it grew too dark to pan for gold. They would need nourishing food after days of cold beans and salt pork on the trail. She was determined to fix a hot meal. She still had the Dutch oven and her cast-iron kettle. Many had been forced to leave such items along the trail to lighten the horrendous drag on wheels and overburdened beasts.

Gathering her pots and utensils, she set out in search of firewood that abounded in the forested area nearby. With the men down at the goldfields, all was still in the camp, leaving only the drone and flutter of late-afternoon insects and birds for company. Quinton had looked so worn and thin as he stood in the swirling river, bending and lifting, sweating beneath the blistering sun. *Let him not be disappointed today,* she prayed.

In the quiet wood, the sun filtered through emerald leaves and made lacy patterns on the ground. The shadows seemed alive—the way they leaped and danced. She drew in her breath. That odd sense of being watched just before she fell asleep changed. The comfort of feeling a caring presence vanished, and in its place came an unsettling fear. She found herself turning to look behind her as she moved, unnerved by the crackle of branches her own steps made.

She chided herself as she collected twigs for the fire. She was no frail, home-loving "little thistle," as her uncle believed she was—as he believed all women were. Still, there was a wildness to this land that demanded respect, if not fear. She began to hum as she filled her apron with brushwood, determined to meet whatever challenges lay ahead.

A sudden snap of twigs behind her brought her bolt upright. Was someone there? Watching her? She shivered in the tepid warmth of the woods, her mind conjuring tales of ravaging animals and attacking Indians. As she backed away, dropping half her load of sticks, a large bird shot out of a thicket, wings flapping in a wild dance. Relief flooded through her. It had been nothing after all. Laughing, she regathered the sticks and headed back to the clearing and the shelter of her wagon.

With her small supply of wood, she got a fire going and hung her pots and pans on a nearby tree for ready access. Cooking in the open was a new and exciting challenge, and she was eager to try her hand at preparing a hot meal without the benefit of a true kitchen. They had enough bacon, potatoes, and dried rutabaga left to make a good supper, but their provisions were small. She hoped they would last until they could purchase more from one of the outfits that serviced the camps from time to time.

She scooped flour from the dwindling supply they had brought in thick, double rucksacks and wondered how the others in their train were faring. Somewhere in the camp, Charity might be cobbling together a meal, though on the trail, she had been unable to raise her head from the pillow. Hannibal had fended for himself and the boy. Perhaps she should invite them to share the evening meal.

You won't get any thanks for your trouble. Constance's warning resurfaced. How sad that Charity turned away human comfort when loneliness and homesickness nagged at them all.

Loneliness settled on her again like a brooding specter as she peered into the woods beyond for some threatening face. The words of the hymn sang in her mind. "Give to the winds thy fears." She would try, but what if . . . ? No, she wouldn't allow herself such speculation.

The approach of riders buoyed her spirit. Quinton and Hoke, mining tools loaded on Ruby's scruffy back, were returning to camp. The stew was ready, its aroma wafting on the breeze. *Perhaps tomorrow I'll try to make biscuits,* she thought as she searched among her utensils for a stew ladle. She must have left it in the wagon. She ran back from her cook tent to the wagon, waving excitedly as the familiar figures drew nearer.

Suddenly, she heard a loud hissing and something rattling nearby. She jumped as the sounds grew louder, more insistent. Transfixed, she looked down at a huge snake coiled in the grass. At the same second, something flew past her head with a whistling rush. An ax. Or a tomahawk? And the writhing snake was still.

She whirled around. Just a few feet away stood an Indian, right arm still poised in the air. Brooding eyes, sculpted mouth set as though in granite, left leg scraping the ground. In an instant, she recognized the crippled young man who had been ordered to collect the gifts the members of the train had offered.

What was he doing here? Were the others coming to attack? Had the crippled brave been the one watching her? The presence that had at first seemed comforting, then made her wary in the woods? Thoughts spun through her head in the space of seconds as she gaped at the tomahawk and the upraised bronzed arm. Whatever he was doing there, whether he had been watching her or not, he had just saved her life.

But suddenly, her brother let out an angry shout and lunged at the young brave, closing the distance between them in seconds. Hoke leaped off his horse, the barrel of his shotgun aimed directly at the Indian's head.

5

Cabot Falls, Vermont
Present Day

*I*t seemed to Sofia that the weekend had flown faster than the speed of light, launching Monday like a long-tailed rocket. It promised to be a full day, and in the evening, her sisters would arrive for dinner and a toast to their beloved Nonna. That meant an Italian dinner with all the trimmings. *Daunting enough*, she thought, but she had promised eight dozen cupcakes to Heather for her fledgling bakery. *What was I thinking?* But true to her word, she'd risen at dawn and stumbled into the kitchen to begin the long day.

In midafternoon, Heather's van appeared in the driveway as Sofia was boxing up the last dozen cupcakes. The coconut macaroons she had also promised were carefully stored in their special tins and ready to transport. She smiled with satisfaction, knowing the word was getting out about her culinary skills. When Heather first went into business, she had begged Sofia to go in with her as a full partner. Like she was some sort of wonder woman who could raise a family of four kids, teach painting classes, *and* help run a full-time baking business.

Thirtysomething and still single, Heather Cookson had bought out a small ice-cream shop in the heart of town and turned it into a bakery. "With a name like mine," she had said, lifting artfully penciled eyebrows and emitting her high-pitched giggle, "what else would I do?"

Surprising everyone who thought she had little but air between her temples, Heather proved something of a management wizard. Business was so good that she had to contract out to supply the burgeoning patronage to her little shop.

Spying her friend through the kitchen window, Sofia pushed damp strands of light brown hair out of her eyes. She glanced despairingly at the kitchen table cluttered with the remains of breakfast and unwanted debris fished from school backpacks. The mess of her cooking added to the chaos. A sprinkling of sugar crunched under her feet. Why did it always look like World War III when she worked on a project?

She drew an exhausted breath. Mondays with four children and a husband to get off to school and work was not for the faint of heart. Of course, it hadn't been her brightest idea to agree to an art lesson at eleven thirty, but Marjorie Bennett had offered to pay double for a second lesson in the space of only a few days. Two bathroom stops and three cookies later, the aging dowager had gone home.

There had been little time to think about the leather pouch tucked in with the drapes. How had it gotten there? Was it really a relic from the nineteenth century?

If only Nonna were alive to explain its appearance. She let her breath out in a weary stream. The novelty of the bag had worn off for Matthew and Luke, who spent Saturday making up games and spinning tales about pirates and treasure. Wynter and Vanessa, consumed with their particular interests, quickly forgot about the find, and she and Jim had just been too busy. She touched a hand to her lower back, which ached with weariness. Time to discover more about the pouch later.

Excited barks from the backyard ended further reflection. Fergus, their border collie, wriggled all over in his efforts to entice Heather to come his way rather than mount the steps to Sofia's back door, as she was now doing.

"Sorry, buddy. Work awaits!" Heather called to him over her shoulder.

Sofia greeted Heather breathlessly after ordering Fergus to be quiet. The black-and-white defender of the household turned with wounded dignity and lay down by the gate, head slunk over his paws.

"He's a charmer, Sofia," Heather said. "And you, my friend, are a lifesaver." She put her head back, nostrils flaring. "Heavenly!" she breathed, bobbing her short, blond curls and favoring Sofia with one of her Cheshire cat grins. "I don't know how you manage it. Between that family of yours and your painting, you are an absolute marvel."

"May Wonder Woman offer you a cup of coffee?" Sofia asked coyly, amused by Heather's comments.

"No thanks, but I'm ordering you to put your feet up and have a cup yourself! You look bushed." Heather whipped out a checkbook, scrawled something on it, and plunked it down on the table. She loaded up the boxes in two special stacking cases and was gone in a whirlwind before Sofia realized that the check Heather had written exceeded their contractual agreement by twenty dollars. A bright spot in the tedium of the hours that lay ahead.

Art tutoring and cupcake baking finished, she managed, with the children's help, to make the house as presentable as possible before her sisters were due to arrive. Ever watchful, they would notice undusted surfaces and grimy corners. As they set their contributions for the dinner on her counter, they would check it first for cleanliness—Rosa openly and Gina covertly.

Sofia went upstairs to her bedroom to finish getting ready for her sisters' visit. Sitting in front of her vanity, she sighed. Would she ever conquer her sense of inferiority where her sisters were concerned? The oldest, Rosa, was an astrophysicist at Cornell University, and next in line, Gina, taught microbiology at Boston University. She, Sofia, was the youngest and, well . . . less accomplished.

Nonna's three granddaughters, whom she had helped raise after the death of their mother, had been close since childhood. Yet Sofia often wondered what genes had rendered her so different, so much less successful than her brilliant sisters.

Jim, her husband and college sweetheart, had told her often enough how proud he was of her for following her creative passion in studio art. He loved that she was a stay-at-home mom for their four children, giving art lessons on the side and creating bakery masterpieces from time to time. *I love it too,* Sofia thought. *Only . . . well, there are just times when I wish I might have pursued something more ambitious.* It didn't help that her sisters were both expert seamstresses like Nonna, while she could barely sew a straight seam.

That's what made it so odd that Nonna had willed the heirloom quilt to her when Rosa was the most obvious, the most qualified candidate. She ran a quick brush through her shoulder-length brown hair, frowning at her reflection in the mirror. *What were you thinking, Nonna?* And yet, possession of the quilt had brought unexpected and sometimes transformative experiences.

She remembered her sisters' horror over finding a hole in the quilt at their last birthday celebration for Nonna. The diary that accompanied the quilt told the exciting story of two Philadelphia sisters who met the famous Annie Oakley featured in Buffalo Bill's Wild West. Free passes to the show were called Annie Oakleys because they looked as though they had been shot through by the sharpshooter's own bullets. They discovered later that the bullet hole had been deliberately worked into the lavender silk square by the quilt's designer.

Sofia was exonerated and faith in her guardianship of the

family heirloom was restored. Well, at least for a while. It didn't stop Rosa and Gina from giving frequent advice on the quilt's proper care and keeping. It was, after all, the tangible reminder of their beloved Nonna and must be protected and preserved at all costs.

Sofia exchanged her flour-dusted jeans and shirt for a pair of slacks and her favorite melon-colored blouse. Jim was entertaining his sisters-in-law to give her time to change her clothes. No doubt he had served a predinner beverage and was recounting the antics of his high school students. *Bless him*, she thought, wondering how she'd been lucky enough to land a husband who put up so admirably with her often-unwieldy family.

She loved her flamboyant, utterly Italian sisters fervently, but keeping peace in the family wasn't always a walk in the park. She gave her lips a hasty touch of Midsummer Melon and entered the living room, where Vanessa was displaying the latest illustrations in her sketchbook. She had shifted from drawing long, lean models in unique costume to interior home design—the more avant-garde the better. Launching into a description of an elegant boudoir, she tossed her shoulder-length blond hair and leaned over her aunt's shoulder.

"The headboard is made entirely of photographs superimposed on pillows and joined together," Vanessa enthused. "Voilà! Not only do you have a comfy backrest for reading or whatever, but while you sleep, you're surrounded by all the people you love the best." Her green eyes glittered in anticipation of her aunt's approval.

Rosa nodded. She was dressed in her usual business suit, this one navy with pinstripes and accented with a crimson blouse. Her black hair was drawn into a chignon at the base of her neck. Elegant and composed, she looked as she might appear before a group of university students. "I've never seen anything quite like it," Rosa said sagely, bending to peer more closely at Vanessa's drawing. "It certainly is different."

"Ugh! Who wants to sleep with all those faces staring down at you?" Wynter said, rolling her eyes in utter distaste. "It could give you nightmares!" Convinced she had the answer to every known problem, Wynter was rarely given to diplomacy. Though younger by two years than Vanessa, she was taller by a head and as dark-haired as her sister was blond. Carrying herself like Roman royalty, she and her aunt Rosa might have been featured on twin Roman coins.

Luke and Matthew sat obediently on the couch, with their father watching from an adjacent chair. Luke had Jim's brown hair and eyes as well as his thoughtful disposition. Like Jim, he was good at fixing things and liked helping his dad with building projects. He probably wasn't deliberately ignoring the home decor discussion or the sarcastic fracas between his sisters. But on the other hand, perhaps he was.

Matthew, true to form, used the occasion of his mom's entrance into the fray by popping up from the couch and throwing his arms around Sofia's waist. In the process, he bumped into the end table, sending the lamp rocking precariously. "Watch out for Aunt Gina's—"

Too late. Gina's glass fell from the end table, spilling the liquid contents onto the rug. It splashed onto her shoes, missing her black sheath dress by an inch.

"Matthew!" Sofia exclaimed. She loved that her rambunctious, hotheaded little boy still warmed to parental hugs and kisses, but sometimes . . . "I'll get a towel."

But Jim popped up and raced into the kitchen. He was back in a flash and tossed a towel to Sofia. What luck that her heroic husband had served white wine rather than red.

"Never mind," Gina said gallantly as Sofia swiped at the wet spot near her left hip. "Better to wear it than drink it, I guess," she said, laughing. "Think of the calories I'll save." The shortest of the sisters and prone to picking up extra pounds, Gina counted calories, usually just before she consumed them.

"I'm so sorry!" Sofia exclaimed as Matthew slunk back in childish embarrassment.

But he beamed when Gina ruffled his hair in a gesture of forgiveness. Sofia promised no further accidents if everyone would gather around the table, which they all did. When Matthew parked himself just to Gina's left, Sofia groaned and gave him a warning look.

Conversation around the table flowed, ebbing and churning as stories mingled with the usual laughter and magnanimity that defined their family. Sofia's lasagna dwindled to a few delectable crumbs. Little remained of the lemon linguini with spinach and prosciutto, which Rosa had brought. Gina had supplied the wine. There were no more mishaps all the way to the Italian ricotta lemon cake with blueberry topping that Sofia had prepared in advance and left to thaw on the counter until—

"Mom, tell Auntie Gina about the bag of gold we found." Matthew's voice rose with excitement.

Rosa and Gina paused their forks in midair to fix Sofia with inquiring stares.

"It's true," Jim said, clearly enjoying the moment. "We struck gold right here in the house." His blue eyes danced as they caught Sofia's.

"Fool's gold in some dumb old sack!" Luke said before stuffing his mouth with a huge bite of lemon cake.

"How do you know it was fool's gold, smarty?" Wynter demanded, elbowing her brother hard enough to knock the fork from his hand. "You got a degree in geology?"

"What *are* they talking about?" Rosa asked, a smile playing around her lips.

Sofia drew in her breath. So much had been going on that she'd barely given the unusual discovery a thought since Saturday.

The box was still under the kitchen table where she'd left it out of sight. "Well," she began, "you know those drapes that always hung in Nonna's house—the red-colored ones with the old-fashioned tiebacks?"

"Ugly as sin!" Gina said. "May Nonna forgive me."

"Well, the kids and I were marking some things for a garage sale on Saturday. We found the drapes Nonna left for me." Sofia paused. "You remember, she thought Jim and I might use them." She shrugged, avoiding the wry expression on Jim's face. He clearly agreed with Gina's assessment of the drapes. "I'd forgotten the box was still down there, but Matthew dragged it up along with the others I marked for the sale. The bag was tucked inside the folds of material. The tag on it had numbers that might be twenty-seven, so it could have something to do with the quilt."

"Ah," said Rosa. "I recall there was something in the diary about panning for gold in California. Some nineteenth-century adventurers heading west. Do you suppose—" She broke off, her dark brows drawn together.

"And there was all this gold inside the bag like real treasure," Matthew quipped.

"We'd love to see it," Rosa said. "Wouldn't we, Gina?"

Sofia shrugged. It was time to adjourn to the four-season room, where they always ended with espresso, which was Jim's department. "Sure, the box is in the kitchen under the table. Vanessa, will you go get the pouch for me?"

When Vanessa returned after several minutes, she held up her hands and shrugged. "Not there," she said simply. "Did you put it somewhere else, Mom?"

"I put it back in the box," she said, surprised. "Wynter? Luke?" she asked mildly.

Their expressions conveyed their confusion. They hadn't touched the box since she had pushed it back under the table, they insisted. Sofia turned to Matthew. Everyone remembered the day Fergus had disappeared, only to show up with Matthew, who had taken their border collie to school for show-and-tell. "You didn't take it to school, did you?"

He shook his curly head vigorously, blue eyes innocent.

Sofia felt a moment of concern, but that was silly. When Jim or the kids mislaid something, she was always summoned like the cavalry to find it. She pushed her chair back. *Am I the only one who can find things around here?* "Let's go have coffee. I'll get the pouch and join you." She turned to Jim, who had risen as well and begun to clear the table. She caught his eye in silent appeal.

"I'll get the espresso going," he said, giving her a warm smile.

"Girls," Sofia said with a nod to Wynter and Vanessa, "I'll check the kitchen and the dining room. You check the rest of the house." *The little pouch has to be here somewhere. Someone must have taken it out to admire it and simply forgotten to put it back.*

She shook out the drapes. She searched every inch of the cardboard box and every nook and cranny in the kitchen and dining room. No sign of the pouch. When Vanessa and Wynter came back empty-handed, Sofia's momentary panic flared into fear. The gold—real or not—was missing. She would have to face her sisters, who would want to know how she could be so careless. How could she be so careless with a nineteenth-century relic?

But who? And why? There must be some logical explanation. Sofia racked her brain, trying to remember just what had occurred since they'd found the bag. Who had been in the kitchen? Her students, Marjorie and Ernest. Both had seen the little pouch. Both had heard Matthew's report of finding gold. *Who else? The furnace guy who'd stood on the porch, looking in the window? Or did someone unknown sneak into the house and take it? But that's ridiculous! The intruder would have been seen, and at night, the security system was armed.*

The whole thing was ridiculous. It couldn't be real gold. But she'd been pretty sure the pouch was authentic nineteenth century and, as such, valuable. And she had lost it. With sinking dread, she went to join her waiting family in the four-season room.

6

Mokelumne Hill, California
September 1849

"No!" Adelia screamed, flailing her arms and attempting to shield the startled brave who had just saved her from the coiled rattlesnake.

Unintelligible sounds flew from Quinton's mouth as he grasped the Indian by the neck and tackled him to the ground. The crack of Hoke's shotgun shattered the air, the blast going mercifully wild.

"Stop. It's not what you think." Adelia gestured wildly at the place where the snake lay with the tomahawk embedded in its body. "Look!"

Quinton and Hoke stared, first at the snake, then at the Indian who scrambled to his feet when Quinton released his hold on him. A heavy silence ensued as though the world had been suspended, and then Quinton ran to his sister, his face ashen. "Are you all right, Addie?" He put his hands on her shoulders, searching her face.

"I'm fine," she said, relief flooding through her. "Thanks to him." She gazed past her brother's head to the Indian who stood motionless, sharp eyes piercing one man, then the other. Adelia ran toward him and held out her hand. "I am in your debt. Please forgive my brother. He didn't know—"

His eyes touched hers briefly, then he looked away. He started to limp toward the snake, probably to retrieve his tomahawk, and more likely to escape the angry white men who'd nearly killed him. When he bent to pick up his weapon, the coarse bangle around his neck dipped forward. An odd assortment of claws and beads and—could it be?—a crucifix?

The Indian stepped backward from the little group, eyes watchful. "Wait," Adelia said. "Please, share our supper. We are—all of us—grateful to you for saving my life." She flung wordless glances of appeal at Quinton and Hoke.

"Yes," Quinton said, "please forgive my hasty reaction. I thought—"

"We both thought to protect the little lady here," Hoke grunted, stroking his beard with fingers that Adelia saw trembled. He'd come close to killing a man, and though he'd likely had to use his gun before, it would go against the grain of this good man who valued life.

There was an odd pause as the Indian and Hoke took each other's measure. Adelia thought she saw something flash between them. Recognition, remembrance? Hoke's gravelly voice broke in. "This here's the lady's brother," he rasped, indicating Quinton. "Quinton Long. We didn't mean no harm."

The Indian brave narrowed his eyes, first at Quinton, then at Adelia, and jerked his head upward. "I am Siba," he said in a proud baritone, startling them all. "I am Cahuilla."

After a second's pause, he bent to retrieve his tomahawk and slipped it into a leather strap on his thigh. As he backed toward the line of trees, his gaze lingered on Adelia. Then he limped away, his left foot making soft swooshing sounds on the hard ground.

She stared after him, amazed. "He speaks English," she whispered. Where had he learned it? And why was he wearing a crucifix among that collection of rude claws? She knew that a dozen years earlier, Spanish missionaries had come to the area, bringing their religion along with practical assistance. Was it then that this young brave had adopted the religion of his teachers? Or, attracted by the shiny bauble, had he simply stolen the crucifix?

But that look in his eyes—half-appealing, half-proud. A tenderness swept through her, replacing her fear. Had the Diggers for whom he had fetched and carried like a slave abandoned him too? She recalled their frightful experience at the end of the trail.

They all stood rigidly rooted to the spot until the raucous call of a crow broke the heavy silence. Likely, the Indian named Siba would not return to the camp unless, like other natives, he hired on at the mines to earn his suppers. His was a proud race, she knew, but the natives were gradually losing their hunting grounds. They had been driven to desperate measures to survive. She vowed to leave some food for him just inside the wooded area behind her wagon.

Muffled shouts and exclamations mingled with the caws of crows as miners returned to the camp with the day's rewards. Feeling Quinton's tug on her arm, Adelia turned to him. Though he looked haggard and spent, his blue eyes shone like beacons. "You fared well today?" she asked.

Pulling a leather poke from his belt, he loosened the string and held it toward her. "Take a look!" he said, beaming with pride. Pea-sized nuggets and smaller flakes of gold glimmered through clay and gravel. "Once all that sediment is cleared, should be as much as fifty dollars." Quinton picked up his slouch hat that had fallen to the ground when he'd charged Siba and slapped Hoke on the shoulder with it. "Hoke here got even more than that. We've found ourselves a good claim, Addie."

"A tolerable day's work," Hoke said. "Ain't no disputing that. But it's all luck, son. One fellow works hard on a claim and gets five dollars a day. The next man, one claim over, is lazier than a three-toed sloth, but he's on a place where the streambed picks up gold, and he makes five hundred in an afternoon. Just plain luck." He cocked his head, listening to the shouts reverberating in the camp.

"We're lucky, and we're going to be even luckier," Quinton said, flinging an arm around Adelia's shoulders. "I just know it. I feel it in my bones."

It was obvious that luck wasn't the only thing he was feeling in his bones. She felt the heavy weight of his arm and realized she was fairly holding him up. He looked terrible. The rigors of the months-long trek from Iowa to California had taken their toll. Could Quinton, accustomed to a life of comparative ease selling hardware in their quiet, civilized town, stand up to the backbreaking work of a prospector?

He had been quiet and contemplative as a child, one who loved to sprawl beneath a chestnut tree with his sketchbook and pencils. His drawings were surprisingly good. She had tried to encourage him. "You could be a great artist someday," she would say. Their mother had coveted his sketches, even the rudest, most elementary, which she hung on the walls of their home and took great pains to point out to any and every hapless visitor.

But life changed when their mother died. Times grew hard, financially and emotionally, and Quinton's hopes to enter university faded with the waning light in Papa's eyes. Father and son worked diligently to keep the hardware business afloat, reserving little time for diversion. With what sadness she had seen the two beloved men in her life come home each night and trudge wearily off to bed after supper.

Adelia sighed. It had been many months since she'd seen Quinton with his sketchbook. She hadn't told him that she'd brought it with them, along with his once-treasured pencils.

Men were returning for the night, some on foot, a few on the backs of horses or mules. They would make bitter coffee and feast on beans or dried pork before stretching out, exhausted, on bedrolls in preparation for the next day's digging. But the day had yielded a harvest of gold, and several men had gathered to swap stories around the fire in the center of the camp and show off their gold.

Ed Hamilton, a thirtysomething schoolteacher with bad eyes, regaled them with accounts of a previously thought dry claim that proved richer than anyone suspected. A Frenchman from Louisiana announced his intention to move on to an even richer vein.

"Best to stay put once you've got a good claim and work it with all you've got," Hoke had counseled Quinton. Adelia had no doubt he was right. Some men wandered the hills and gulches, dreaming of the next big strike rather than toiling for gold. These drifters looked for undiscovered gravel where they could simply pluck up nuggets and earn five hundred a day. She was glad Quinton had agreed to remain on their plot of ground and see what it might yield.

In the three days since arriving at the Mokelumne, their efforts had yielded close to one hundred fifty dollars in gold dust. From most accounts, their neighbors were finding success as well. She scanned the group of toil-worn men whose faces remained unshaven, their drab clothes unwashed. But their elation was palpable. Happily, they spoke of their families back home, occasionally turning misty-eyed.

"You put them in mind of their wives and sweethearts," Hoke told her. "Some of them ain't seen nothing soft or beautiful in a coon's age."

Adelia looked down at her faded calico dress, the red, chapped hands gripping the battered coffeepot. She felt far from soft and beautiful. What would Augustus Harte think if he should see her now? Her mind filled with a vision of him—tall, resplendent in his uniform, boots shining. She imagined his voice, mellow with affection as he led her onto the dance floor at the small military soiree hosted in Kanesville two years before. As unused to dancing as she, he had moved fluidly but cautiously, his hand warm at her waist.

"It's very strange," he had said softly later when they strolled around the courtyard. "Strange how a moment in your life becomes so important." He had paused before adding, "A whole month or a year can go by, bringing nothing of significance, and then you meet someone . . ."

He had looked deeply into her eyes. "No indigo sea could match them for vibrant color." Then his gaze had fallen away. Why did he say such things? They dropped from his lips like poetry, and she knew it was unwise to trust so honeyed a tongue. He was to leave the next morning, and she had been breathless, wondering, waiting. Tomorrow lay between them—without promise, harsh and unyielding. There was a war on, after all. Though she'd never found his name among the fallen, she couldn't be sure that he was even alive.

Why couldn't she dismiss these adolescent memories from her past? Augustus was long gone. Whatever had happened to him, he clearly had no interest in her. She imagined his warm amber eyes turned toward a delicate wife and rosy-cheeked children.

"Make sure those embers are crushed when you're done with all this foolish celebrating."

Adelia spun around to see Wylie Hunter staring sternly down at her. He looked every bit the gentleman. Unlike the other miners, he had shaved his beard, leaving only a black mustache above his full lips. The flannel shirt beneath a leather vest was surprisingly clean. He tipped his broad, high hat that made him seem even taller than his imposing six feet. His dark brows lifted slightly, and Adelia thought a hint of a smile touched his eyes before quickly disappearing.

She'd accustomed herself to Wylie's arrogant manner, which hadn't changed since the wagon train had disbanded upon reaching their destination. He had set himself as a kind of watchman, imposing rules for proper conduct in mining camps, and had chosen to settle off by himself farther down the Mokelumne. He avoided gatherings in which miners boasted of their claims, swapped stories, and in general enjoyed company after long days of digging and panning.

"He ain't much for mixing," Hoke had said one day, raising his bushy eyebrows. "Got his britches yanked up higher than a long-tailed kite."

Adelia didn't like Wylie's parental attitude, and she wasn't so foolish as to leave a campfire untended. "Of course," she said, forgoing a caustic comment, and managed a smile. Perhaps, knowing their limited knowledge of outdoor living, he only meant to keep them all safe.

He was watching her through coal-dark eyes, something urgent burning in their depths. When his horse began to stamp impatiently, Wylie drew on the reins and gave an upward jerk of his head to signal his imminent departure. "And you'd be wise to keep that Indian away from your tents and our claims," he said darkly.

Adelia stared after his departing form. What Indian? What had he seen? She walked several paces toward the forest where she had seen Siba depart. Wylie must have seen him too. Though there was no sign of the strange brave with the crucifix, she was pleased to see that the plate of stew she'd left for him on a fallen log was empty. Empty and wiped clean.

She walked back to her wagon, pondering the strange Indian brave named Siba. She was so deep in thought that she barely heard Hannibal Reed's voice. "Evening to you," he said solemnly.

She nodded. But he was looking past her to Wylie Hunter riding off in the distance. Hannibal's severe features seemed to grow harder. "You'd be wise to beware of that man," he said solemnly.

She cocked her head at him, surprised. In the last few minutes, two men had deigned to impart their "wisdom"— Wylie warning about Siba and now Hannibal advising caution concerning Wylie. Hannibal, she had learned, seldom saw silver linings in any cloud and was quick to pass judgment. He'd left a farm in Kentucky after a series of heavy crop losses and the death of his little girl. Isaac, the lanky boy at his side, shuffled his feet and looked around nervously, as though he might run off if opportunity allowed.

It was rumored in the camp that Isaac's mother, Charity, rarely left her bed. After a day of work coaxing gold from rock and water, Hannibal had to see to his own needs and those of his boy. "I hope Charity is better this evening." Adelia ventured tentatively.

The eyes of both father and son dropped away. Hannibal fidgeted with his slouch hat, which he held flat against his canvas trousers. "She suffers," Hannibal replied in a low voice, eyes narrowed. "But the Almighty will have his way." Then, handing the boy a covered pan that likely served as a chamber pot, he jerked his head toward the woods. "Go along now," he told him grimly.

Adelia's heart ached for the little family and especially for Isaac, who dutifully trotted off toward the woods. She had an elixir of herbs that might prove helpful to Charity if she was still ailing, but what tonic could heal a broken spirit?

After finishing the plate of stew that Adelia had concocted from bacon, potatoes, and rutabaga, Quinton, practically asleep on his feet, went to bed. Adelia watched him crawl into his tent, then, using the method her brother had instructed, she sat near the fire to wash the remaining sediment from the precious metal, which she would store in her wagon in a feed sack under her pillow. No one seemed concerned that their gold would be stolen. The miners were honorable men—family men intent on making a strike and returning to their wives and children.

It gave Adelia an odd sense of pride in her fellow "forty-niners"—as they had come to be called—in spite of the little voice in her mind that couldn't quite believe such virtue could long endure. *What lies behind us and what lies before us are small matters compared to what lies within us,* she thought, recalling the sage words.

Perhaps because the goldfields were huge and new strikes were being found almost daily, it didn't make sense to steal when gold could be plucked up without risk. Punishment for an offense could be swift and without any real due process of law. She had heard of a prospector jumping another man's claim who was lashed and driven out of a camp. A miners' court could impose harsh justice: confiscation of claims, banishment, thirty lashes, even hanging. In the absence of formal law, the miners' own quick and relentless version served admirably.

Hoke returned from bedding down Ruby with the miners' horses and oxen in the rude corral that also held their prized milk cow. He approached Adelia's cook tent, shoulders slumped with weariness. He doffed his battered slouch hat and nodded toward Quinton's tent. "He's plumb tuckered. But happy, I reckon."

Adelia held out a tin cup filled with chicory coffee. "Hoke, what do you know about that Indian we met earlier—Siba, I mean?"

Hoke leaned forward on the pine log seat. He peered into the fire, his gray chin whiskers jutting forward, and was silent.

"I thought I saw something pass between you back there when he killed the snake," she ventured when it seemed he might not have heard her. "Like maybe you'd met before."

"The war. That's what we got in common," Hoke said in a low voice tinged with sadness.

As scout for the army, Hoke must have seen the horrors of war firsthand, Adelia thought. She had lost a cousin in the Mexican-American War that pitted a politically divided and militarily unprepared Mexico against the expansionist-minded administration of U.S. President James K. Polk. Polk believed the United States was destined to spread across the continent to the Pacific. When the dust cleared, Mexico had lost a third of its territory, including California, Utah, Nevada, Arizona, and New Mexico. And countless mothers had lost their sons.

"The Temecula Massacre of '47," Hoke continued after some moments. "We both fought the Luiseño, fierce enemies of the Cahuilla. When his own tribe turned him out, Siba was raised by missionaries. He learned the white man's ways." Hoke wiped a dribble of coffee from his mouth on the sleeve of his shirt. "The wound he got never healed right. Guess he's been foraging around these parts since the war just trying to stay alive."

Adelia shook her head, trying to imagine the struggle Siba faced. "He took the plate of food I left for him," she said. "I wish there was something we could do to really help him."

"We were talkin', Quinton and me, while all the jawin' was going on at the fire," Hoke said tentatively. "Back along the Calaveras, Indians hire on to rich claims. Eight dollars a day is the going rate for white hired workers, but the Indians just work for food. Siba could help us if he's a mind to." He set down his empty cup and stood abruptly. "Beholden," he said, nodding his shaggy head, and left her.

Wylie Hunter's words rang in her mind. *Keep that Indian*

away from your tents—and our claims. If Siba had a mind to stay and work with Quinton and Hoke, the self-appointed guardian of the camp wouldn't like it at all.

7

Cabot Falls, Vermont
Present Day

*W*hen Jim left for work and the children for school, Sofia lingered at the kitchen table. She poured herself another cup of coffee and considered her options for the day. She had an order for a simple sheet cake with vanilla frosting, art classes to arrange, and considerable cleanup after the weekend and Monday's dinner with Rosa and Gina. But the loss of the pouch lay heavily on her mind, especially as she recalled her sisters' criticism upon learning that a potentially valuable nineteenth-century relic had been lost. How could she have been so careless?

"It should have been sold to a historical society the minute it was discovered, Sofia," Rosa had said, drawing her shapely brows together in frustration. "Or you could have named your price on the private market."

The discovery of the pouch had been startling enough. Who would expect to open a box of faded old drapes and find a pouch of gold—or something that looked like gold? And then to discover it gone. They had searched the house from top to bottom, considered every family scenario, but there was no denying it. The pouch was gone.

Gina, often gentler in her comments, had wondered if the quilt was still in its place, still intact. Sofia couldn't blame her. Anything to do with Elena's legacy was a priority. She had gone upstairs to check on the heirloom and assured them all was well. She had brought the journal back downstairs, and together, they had begun to read the tales from the Gold Rush of 1849, penned by a woman named Adelia Long.

Whether the pouch contained real gold or not, she had to find out what happened to the little bag. "You should report it missing, honey," Jim had said that morning before kissing her good-bye. Sofia knew it was the right thing to do. It was, after all, a potentially valuable relic, as Rosa had so succinctly pointed out. She gave the kitchen a lick and a promise and then went in search of Officer Ryan Quimby.

It wasn't her first foray into the realm of crime fighting. The people of Cabot Falls were, in general, honest, kind, generous, and hardworking. They embraced the town's natural beauty, its sparkling lakes, rambling woodlands, and majestic peaks. But some unsavory characters did occasionally despoil the scene. And there had been occasions for Sofia to ply her analytical skills in the interest of justice.

The adventures on which she had embarked usually included her best friends, both fellow painters. Marla Dixon, a widow in her late forties, was quiet by nature but full of zest. She worked at the Cabot Falls Library and was guiding a son through the treacherous waters of his teen years. Marla's lean athletic build testified to her love of the outdoors, which was often reflected in her paintings. She and Sofia, along with Julie Butler, had quickly become friends and formed a group called the Pinot Painters. They met weekly to create and share one another's burdens.

Julie Butler, chatty and boisterous, was in her early forties and had twin daughters. Besides her family duties and her full-time work in marketing at a public relations firm, Julie still had energy to spare for extracurricular activities. Sofia depended on her wit and fire. She had made a date for lunch with Julie, but first, she would advise Officer Quimby of the latest mystery in the Parker household.

Sofia liked the straightforward young man with his broad, open-faced smile. He'd grown up in Cabot Falls, and now, at thirty, his training behind him, he had returned to the town he so clearly loved. He was studying for a forensics degree and had great ambitions, but he also took his job of small-town peacekeeping very seriously. Sofia felt honored to call him her friend.

"Sofia Parker! A pleasure to see you, as always," Ryan said, rising and extending his hand. Of medium height, he wasn't a big man but solidly built with a shock of ginger-colored hair and boyish freckles. He smiled warmly, indicated a chair for his guest, and sat down across from her. Hazel eyes probing, he rubbed his jaw thoughtfully. "What brings you in on a Tuesday morning?"

"A rather strange event, I'm afraid," Sofia said with a sigh. "I guess I'm here to report a robbery."

He said nothing but raised his eyebrows to indicate he was listening.

"A bag of gold—or what looks like gold," she said, studying her folded hands briefly. "You're aware that my Grandmother Baresi left a family heirloom with me, a very special quilt that has considerable historical significance."

Quimby leaned forward in his chair. "Yes, I've had the opportunity to see it."

"Well, she also left a battered-looking antique leather pouch, which I found quite by accident. It was wrapped up with some old drapes that she thought I might want to hang in my living room." Sofia looked up sheepishly. "We never cared for them and set them aside for a garage sale. Going through stuff last Saturday, folded in the drapes was this pouch with what looked like gold inside." She briefly outlined the connection to the quilt and the suspicion that the pouch that had disappeared might be a true nineteenth-century relic.

Ryan pursed his lips and rubbed his jaw again. "Whew. That's quite a story. I assume you've cross-examined your family to make sure someone didn't just mislay it or—"

"Absolutely," she said, interrupting. She let her breath out in a slow sigh. "Jim and I have racked our brains trying to figure out what could have happened to it. So much was going on. We were all busy, and I had art students to attend to. So, I just tucked the pouch back inside the box with the drapes and scooted it under the kitchen table."

"I'm sure you've considered who was in your house at the time. Those art students, who were they?"

Sofia described Ernest Haynes, the investor with dreams of becoming the next Picasso, and Marjorie Bennett, the Georgia O'Keefe aspirant with the gossipy tongue. "Both of them came into the kitchen at the crucial moment." She paused. "Then there was the furnace maintenance man. Our house was something of a madhouse on Saturday."

"I can imagine," Ryan said knowingly. As a guest in their home several times, he was well acquainted with Sofia's active children, who all loved him. "I'll need names and addresses."

"I just hate accusing anyone." She bit her lip. "But someone must have slipped into the kitchen and stolen it. I don't know when exactly. It wasn't discovered missing until after dinner last night when I went to show it to my sisters."

"We'll check it out," Ryan said decisively and gave her an encouraging smile. "We may have to tread carefully where Mr. Haynes is concerned. He has quite a standing in the community, and he hardly needs the money." He rolled his expressive eyes. "Picasso, huh?"

Sofia rolled hers in concert and waved good-bye. "Let me know anything you find out."

"You do the same."

Realizing she had spent a bit longer with Officer Quimby than planned, Sofia hurried to the Cosmos Café to meet Julie. It was a cool prespring day, and melting snow trickled down the gutters in a glimmering stream. She shivered and zipped up her fleece hoodie.

"There you are!" Julie announced when Sofia slid into the booth. She flipped her red hair off her left shoulder with brightly enameled fingers. Today her nails were painted with perfectly shaped roses and tiny green leaves. Julie treated fingernail painting as an art form. Her eyes were wide, green circles as she commanded Sofia's gaze. "How'd it go with the police?"

She had filled in both of her best friends on the pouch of gold and its subsequent loss. Marla and Julie were often ports in the storm, filling a place that family members could not. "I gave him the details, and he's going to look into it," Sofia said wearily. "I just don't understand it. Who would do something like this?"

"It certainly is a puzzle, but it's very exciting. Imagine, a piece of genuine Gold Rush history!" Julie pointed to a line in her menu. "I'm having the mushroom burger. How about you? I ordered you an iced tea. That's right, isn't it?" Sofia found Julie's repartee comforting, and she began to relax. She seconded Julie's order for a mushroom burger and stirred an extra teaspoon of sugar into her tea. Comfort food was definitely in order.

"I think we should go see that nosy Marjorie Bennett," Julie said as Sofia was about the attack the second half of her burger. "The boutique where she works is just around the corner. You know how she loves flashy things. Maybe she saw gold and couldn't help herself."

"Hmm," Sofia mused. It didn't seem likely, and yet, Marjorie had been in the Parker house and made more than one excuse to use the restroom. Sofia couldn't imagine what to say or how she would go about questioning the elderly woman. Still, it was a start, and she had to do something. She drew in her breath. "We're probably out of our minds, but let's go."

Minding the boutique was a tall, willowy woman with black hair into which had been worked a broad white strip. *Rather like a skunk*, Sofia couldn't help thinking. "We're looking for Marjorie Bennett. Is she in today?"

"I've been filling in for *someone* the last three days," she said with a nasal twang. "Maybe it's her. I really wouldn't know." She fiddled with a quirky scarf at her neck. "Is there anything I can show you today? We have some to-die-for new accessories from Madam Collier."

Sofia and Julie made quick apologies and left. Once out, Julie rolled her eyes. "You think that hairstyle will catch on?"

"Maybe in the animal kingdom," Sofia said and paused midstep. "Three days. Do you suppose Marjorie's sick?" *Sick or skipped town with the booty?* Sofia wondered. "Maybe we should go see her at home. Do you have time?"

Julie, always up for an adventure, was more than willing, as Sofia expected. They drove to a quiet street at the south end of Cabot Falls where fences surrounded midsize homes that had likely been built in the 1980s. With most people at work or school, there were few signs of life. No car was parked outside number 414, which Marjorie had listed as her address when she signed up for art classes.

"Name's right there on the mailbox," Julie offered, opening the front gate. The two walked up the short path to the front door and rang the bell. No sound ushered from inside after several rings and urgent raps on the door.

"Look at the newspapers on the porch—three of them," Sofia said.

"Why would anyone do that?" Julie wrinkled her short nose. "It's a clear invitation to thieves that no one's home."

But what if Marjorie was too ill to bring in her newspapers? Sofia swallowed, warding off a sense of dread.

"Let's try the back," Julie said, descending the porch steps in a quick bounce. She grabbed Sofia's hand, and together, they circled around to the rear where they came to yet another fence.

"It seems Miss Marjorie is a mite overprotective of her property," Sofia said as she lifted the latch on the wrought iron gate and suddenly froze.

A snarling ball of black fur and gleaming fangs lunged forward, straining at a long chain that did not restrict passage to the fence. Growling and baring angry teeth, the animal rose high on its back legs and put two enormous front paws on the gate.

They leaped back and ran to Sofia's car as the furious barking echoed through the quiet street. Not waiting to see if neighbors had stepped out to investigate the furor, they sped away.

"I think I might lose my lunch," Julie said.

"Take a deep breath," Sofia advised sagely, though her own heart raced like a runaway train. Seeing a neighborhood park, she pulled in and stopped the car. "I didn't know Marjorie had a dog," Sofia said quietly after a few seconds to catch her breath.

"Was that a dog? I thought it was a wolf with a chain saw." Julie clasped her arms over her stomach and laughed with relief.

Sofia laughed too. It was funny, in spite of the fact that they might have been its supper. "I'm sorry I got you into this. You all right?"

"Aged by two years, but I'm just ducky, thank you. No, really, I'll be fine, and you didn't force me to go. I was as curious as you. What do you think is going on?"

"Well, for one thing, I'm going to report this to Officer Quimby," Sofia said.

"Don't forget to warn him about the beast," Julie said with a grin. She swept her red hair off her forehead. "Now where should we go?" Julie was not about to give up a good adventure.

"I'm going to take you back to the Cosmos Café so you can retrieve your car and get back to work," she said firmly. "Then I'm going home where sanity reigns."

"Killjoy!"

After dropping Julie off, Sofia headed home, wondering about Marjorie Bennett. If she had stolen the pouch from the box of drapes, what did she possibly hope to gain by hiding out? She wasn't a stupid woman. She wouldn't know if the gold inside was real or fake. Perhaps her mysterious disappearance meant nothing at all. Or she was ill or had just gone to visit a friend, forgetting to stop the paper and leaving the dog to guard the house. *But if Marjorie isn't the guilty party, then what has happened to Nonna's mysterious treasure?*

When she got back to the house, Jim stood at the door, watching her alight from her car. His day started early and ended when the last of his classes was finished. Sofia liked the occasions when he came home early and they could have a cup of coffee together before the children came home. She never tired of seeing his lean, well-balanced physique, whether in dress shirt and slacks or in his comfortable khakis and flannel shirt as he appeared now. His blond hair that tended to curl when it grew long was slightly rumpled, his expression worried. As she approached, she saw that he had a newspaper in his hand.

"Hi," she called, hurrying up the steps to give him a quick hug. But something in his demeanor stopped her. She looked up into uncharacteristically clouded blue eyes.

He held out the newspaper, folded in half, and stepped back into the house. Sofia followed, her eyes catching on a headline, "Gold Strike in Cabot Falls Home." Then she saw a familiar name—theirs!

"A valuable pouch connected to the California Gold Strike of 1849 has been found in the home of James and Sofia Parker."

She gasped and read on.

"It is not known if the contents of the pouch are authentic, but sources reveal the item was discovered by chance and may have been secreted in its hiding place for more than 150 years."

"How? Who?" Sofia stammered, wide-eyed.

"I thought you might know," Jim said, shaking his head.

"I haven't told anyone except Ryan Quimby, and that was just today." She paused. Well, she had told Marla and Julie, but neither of them would violate the Parkers' privacy. "This is outrageous." *Marjorie!* Sofia thought. *It's the kind of thing Marjorie Bennett, talebearer extraordinaire, might do.* In fact, she once worked for the newspaper's "About Town" section.

Jim scratched his head thoughtfully and sighed with exasperation. "Three people have called since I came home—two wanting to sign up for art classes and somebody else wanting you to bake a wedding cake. It seems you may have attained celebrity status."

The front door flew open, and ten-year-old Matthew came bounding in, flung his book bag down, and announced proudly, "Everyone wants me to bring the pouch of gold to school for show-and-tell tomorrow!"

When the phone suddenly rang, Sofia and Jim looked at each other and simultaneously leaped to disconnect it.

8

Mokelumne Hill, California
September 1849

*T*hree days after Quinton had nearly killed Siba, thinking he was attacking her, Adelia woke with a start. She peered under the wagon's canvas flap to see dawn breaking the heavy drape of darkness. She'd been asleep only a few hours. When she'd last checked on Quinton, he'd been sleeping, but it was a fitful sleep brought on as much by the laudanum she'd administered as from his illness. But at least he had found some relief from the coughing that had plagued him.

When Hoke had brought him back to camp tied onto Ruby's back, Quinton had been too weak to hold himself in the saddle, let alone stand. Hoke had met Adelia's grave eyes. "Powerful sorry," he had said and carefully had set the sick man on his cot. He'd stood looking down at the face that was flushed with fever. "He should have stopped days ago, but he wouldn't quit." Hoke had shaken his shaggy head. "The boy's stubborn as a two-headed mule with a thistle stuck in his foot."

Adelia had rushed to apply cool water to her brother's head and thrashing limbs. The illness that had began while they were still on the trail had worsened. His strength depleted in the difficult passage from Iowa to California, he had allowed himself no time to rest but had thrown himself into the business of mining with feverish determination. Even for Quinton, the promise of riches had been all-consuming.

Using her arsenal of herbs and cures, Adelia treated her brother's symptoms as best she could, praying it would be enough. She couldn't be sure what was wrong with him, nor was there a doctor in the camp. *What if he were to die in this place, far from home and family?*

Dropping the canvas flap, she flew from her wagon bed to Quinton's tent. He was moaning softly in a semistupor and tossing amid bedclothes damp with sweat. Adelia put her hand to his forehead and tried to convince herself that his fever had diminished a little. *My poor little man,* she lamented without sound, remembering how she had comforted her brother when he was small.

She had always been the one to take care of him after their mother died, though Adelia was a mere child herself. When he was ten, he'd contracted rheumatic fever, a condition that often left patients with a weakened heart. Adelia had kept an almost constant vigil, preparing poultices and rubbing his legs. He lay in bed day after day for months, trying desperately not to cry, but she knew he was nearly frantic with pain. To distract him she would read to him—*Tales of the Arabian Nights, The Count of Monte Cristo,* all the swashbuckling adventure stories he loved.

"My poor little man," she had soothed him then, giving little thought to her own fifteen-year-old pursuits. As he gradually grew better, she tutored him in his studies, working far into the night to catch up with the demands of her own education. Quinton had been lucky then. His heart had remained strong, but she knew he was left with a legacy of arthritic pain, which standing for hours in the cold waters of the Mokelumne could only exacerbate.

Adelia shook her head to clear it of old memories. She put a cup of water mixed with horseradish root and honey to her brother's lips. She'd used the mixture to nurse fellow forty-niners who had become ill on the trail. The herb was known to stimulate the body's immune system and soothe inflamed muscles. *Please, please, let it work for Quint,* she prayed.

He tossed his head from side to side before taking a few sips. "Addie," he rasped, "I'm sorry . . ."

"Hush," she said, dipping the flannel into a basin near his cot and wiping his forehead. Fair hair that had grown too long on the trail curled softly like a child's and wisped across his red-rimmed eyes. As she smoothed his hair back, a lump caught in her throat. "It's going to be all right," she whispered.

But was it going to be all right? How long would it be before he could do a day's work? If ever? Her thoughts horrified her. She'd seen stronger men than Quinton die from what she feared was the dreaded influenza. She continued to talk in soft, encouraging tones, telling him not to worry, but dark visions raged on in her mind.

What would they do? How would they support themselves if Quinton couldn't pan for gold? Such dreams they had of making enough money for a new start, a new enterprise that would make Papa proud. But would they now have to seek passage on the next available wagon train and go home empty-handed? Would they have to depend on the mercies of Uncle Edward and Aunt Felicity? She mustn't think the worst. She must believe Quinton would get well. She would believe for him and for herself.

She knew Quinton worried that someone would take over his carefully staked-out claim. A man held his claim by leaving his tools on it. If he didn't show up for a month, it was assumed he had abandoned it, and anyone could then take ownership.

"I'll keep my eyeballs peeled," Hoke told her. "Anyone tries to jump that claim, I'll get on 'em like ugly on an ape."

Gently, she exchanged clean linens from her own bed for Quinton's soiled ones and doubled a bedroll under his shoulders to keep his head elevated. "You just rest," Adelia whispered. "You'll feel better in a few days." When he began breathing more evenly, she left his tent quietly to greet the uncertain day.

Stumbling into the early light with her load of linens, she was surprised to see a man bending over her fire pit, his back to her, coaxing firewood into flame. Like the other men in camp, he wore canvas trousers and a faded flannel shirt, which had the sleeves torn out to reveal muscular brown arms. Long black hair streamed to his shoulders beneath a raglike bandana. It was several moments before she recognized who was tending her fire. Siba.

Quinton and Hoke had alternately hired Siba to work their claims, but the Indian had stayed out of sight of the camp. *A wise move*, Adelia thought. But it saddened her that he should be considered a threat, even though he had been educated at a white mission school, scouted for the army during the Mexican-American War, and could likely outsmart any white miner. To Wylie Hunter, who oversaw everything that happened at the camp known now as Mok Hill, Siba was definitely persona non grata.

At the sound of her footsteps, Siba straightened. He turned, sharp eyes watchful, sleeveless shirt unbuttoned. The necklace with its complement of claws and crucifix gleamed against his bronzed chest.

Adelia smiled to show him he was welcome, but also because she recognized the shirt as Quinton's. It was no doubt her brother's ploy to make Siba appear less Indian and fit in with the other miners.

"Thank you for kindling the fire for me," she said, touched by his kindness. She shifted the load in her arms, nodded toward the wagon, where they would be less visible to prying eyes, and indicated that he should follow. His eyes darted back to Quinton's tent, concern in their dark depths. "The young one—he is better?"

Adelia placed the load of soiled linen on the ground and sat down on a hollowed-out log where she often rested in the evening and watched the stars wink in the heavens. California mornings were no less spectacular when the sun climbed over the Sierras at dawn. She never tired of the majesty and wonder of the open skies. Another "chair" had been hewn and placed across from her resting place.

"Please," she said, gesturing for Siba to sit. "I'm afraid my brother is not well," she said when Siba sat, his injured leg stretched awkwardly in front of him. She kept her voice low, lest they be overheard.

She found his reference to "the young one" interesting, since Siba could hardly be much older than Quinton. But perhaps he, too, saw the vulnerable quality in her brother that made people want to protect him: Quinton's dreamy tenderness of eye, the childlike delight as well as unfeigned moments of despair. *Is it the artist in him?* she had often wondered. But art had been swallowed up in his eagerness for gold.

"His fever is not yet controlled, and his cough robs him of rest," she added, feeling the heavy weight of her own words.

"I am sorry," he said, casting his eyes to the ground.

They sat silently for long moments, hearing only the flutter and chirp of early birds. She studied her companion through intermittent glances. *An unusual man,* she thought. *No guttural half words, no fractured pronouns. He has learned the white man's language well.*

Hoke had told her that Siba was orphaned as a child and raised by Spanish missionaries—in particular, a certain Sister Gwendolyn, whom he said bore some resemblance to Adelia. She remembered how Siba had stared at her that first day when he was fetching and carrying for the band of Indians who stopped their train. She recalled how he had watched out for her that first morning in camp and saved her from the dangerous snake.

"What happened to Chapter?" she asked in a small voice. "Sister Gwendolyn."

At the sound of the name, Siba's jaw clenched, and a shadow passed over his features. He did not look at her. Long seconds passed. Perhaps he would not respond. When he spoke again, his voice was raspy, almost too low to hear. "The sickness. I think your people call it cholera." He paused, and his jaw slackened. "She was a good woman. Like you."

The word "cholera" struck fear in Adelia's heart, overbalancing the surprise of Siba's compliment. She was reasonably certain that Quinton was not suffering from the dreaded disease that had taken so many lives among the forty-niners and people back home. Many gold seekers traveling west feared attack by Indian bands, but that seldom happened. Instead, diseases were the biggest killers: cholera, mountain fever, pneumonia, and diphtheria. Many gold seekers succumbed and were buried along the trail.

Siba broke into her dire thoughts. "I will watch over the young one's claim," he said and rose suddenly from the log, swinging his crippled leg in a kind of arc. "I will go now."

"Siba!" Adelia said urgently, rising too. "You must be very careful." Foreigners were becoming more and more vulnerable among white miners. Indians especially. She thought of Wylie and his warning but stopped herself from uttering his name.

Siba turned back to look at her intently. "I will watch for Hawk Eyes," he said.

He must have read my mind, she thought, knowing that "Hawk Eyes" was Siba's nickname for Wiley.

Siba stood silent for several seconds before speaking again. "May the Great Spirit watch out for you and the young one." And with that, he moved away more rapidly than she thought possible.

The sun had crested the Sierras as Adelia began the task of baking biscuits. When Hoke returned from the diggings, he would have something better than hardtack and beans to eat. And she would reserve a few biscuits for Quinton in case he was well enough for solid food. The flour wouldn't last much longer, but the supply wagon was expected to come through camp soon. She hoped she had enough gold to purchase what they needed.

What are we going to do? As she sat on the old three-legged stool, stirring the batter for biscuits, she struggled to tamp down her anxiety. Uncle Edward's words rang through her mind: *I've read the reports, boy. And I haven't missed the ones that tell of men coming back broken in health and spirit, and all for the lure of easy money.*

Maybe she could don boots and pantaloons and dig for gold like the Frenchwoman she had seen standing in Angel's Creek, dipping and pouring water into the washer, which her husband was rocking. Day after day she worked quietly and steadily in her old Panama hat, performing her share of the gold-digging labor.

How long could she stand up to it? Digging down to bedrock, freezing her legs in water, poking coyote holes into gravel, climbing hills. She cringed. She wasn't cut out for such work. *It appears Quint isn't either,* she thought sadly.

She turned six golden biscuits out into a metal bowl and watched the fragrant steam rise in the morning air. Engrossed in her dark ruminations, she wasn't aware that a man was standing a few feet away in a grimy slouch hat, holding a wooden plate in rough fingers.

"Name's John Stoughton, and I'll give you five dollars for them biscuits," he said.

She stared up at the miner. He was a new arrival, one in a stream of gold seekers arriving almost daily. He was probably in his fifties, his beard a rangy brown streaked with gray. Deep wrinkles embedded with dirt surrounded his watery blue eyes.

She stammered in surprise as he pulled a pouch from his belt and opened the string. Perhaps thinking she was about to refuse, he spoke again. "Ten!" he said. "I'll give you ten pinches for 'em." He held the pouch out for her to extract the gold dust.

Quickly, Adelia turned the biscuits onto the man's rough-hewn dish, then took a few pinches of gold dust. He had offered ten. Was it right to accept so much? He pressed the pouch forward, urging her to take the full ten pinches. She dropped them into her tin cup. Before she had taken the last pinch, John Stoughton had swallowed two biscuits and was practically groaning with satisfaction at their savory goodness.

"Them tastes just like home," he mumbled through mouthfuls. "I'll be back tomorrow, and I'll be thanking you kindly."

Adelia glanced into the tin cup. *Ten dollars for six biscuits!* Would miners really pay for home cooking? Why hadn't she thought of it before? Very few men knew how to cook. Most survived on cold beans, hardtack, and whatever game they might have energy to hunt and roast over an open fire. But she had her pots and utensils and her cookstove. There were other ways to make money besides digging in the ground, and these miners flush with newfound wealth were willing to pay. Papa would be so proud.

That's my clever girl. She could almost hear his words breaching time and space. He had always applauded her successes as heartily as she sought his approval. Now, looking down at Stoughton's gold dust, she felt the elation of it digging deep into her soul. As quickly, she recalled the words that often followed Papa's approbation: *It's good to be clever but great to be good.*

A noise from behind startled her. Plates and pots crashing to the ground. Turning, she caught sight of someone streaking away from the campsite into the devouring woods.

9

Cabot Falls, Vermont
Present Day

Sofia and Jim managed to restore a sense of normalcy to their household after reading the newspaper article and fending off curious callers. But sleep had come slowly for Sofia.

Now it was morning. Sofia sent the last Parker—Wynter—off to catch the school bus, arranged for morning coffee with Marla, and headed for the police department. She had advised Ryan Quimby of Marjorie Bennett's seeming disappearance and was eager to know if he had learned anything further.

When she reached the Cabot Falls Police Department, she found two officers working away at computers while a middle-aged receptionist in regular attire greeted her, curiosity plain on her round face.

"I'd like to see Officer Quimby," Sofia said.

"He's out on a call. Perhaps you'd like to wait?" She raised a penciled brow and surveyed Sofia through penetrating brown eyes.

"Sure." Sofia sat down to wait under the watchful eye of the receptionist, who, along with the rest of Cabot Falls, had likely read the account in the newspaper. Theirs was a quiet, hardworking community with little scandal: an occasional drunk-and-disorderly charge, usually during the tourist season, or a rare property dispute. Not much excitement interrupted their ordinary days, unless you counted the mysteries she had found herself embroiled in since taking on the secrets of the quilt.

What is it about the prospect of gold that turned hearts so quickly? Like Adelia Long, her brother, and the other hopefuls in the journal. What made them borrow money, mortgage property, or spend their life savings in pursuit of the kind of wealth they had never dreamed of before? Sofia had to admit it was exciting, but she couldn't help wishing Nonna hadn't given her the elusive treasure wrapped up in old drapes and that they could just get back to their pleasant, everyday life.

Voices rang out suddenly from the front door of the station. First, a high-pitched wailing, and then a calmer voice, which she recognized as Ryan's. She got up, training her eyes on the door, which opened with a rush of wind.

"Please, step inside," Officer Quimby said, holding the door to usher someone in.

A tearful Marjorie Bennett stepped over the threshold, teetering on heels much too high for an elderly lady to wear safely. "I didn't do anything," she whined, clutching at the collar of her bright magenta coat. Tendrils of her silver hair hung loose around a pallid face sporting two bright spots of rouge. Darkly circled brown eyes spoke either of disturbed mascara or too little sleep. "This is all a misunderstanding," she wailed. "I wasn't hiding from the police!" Spying Sofia, her complexion paled even more.

Officer Quimby took Marjorie firmly by the arm. "Come now, Mrs. Bennett. Let's go where we can talk." He jerked his head toward Sofia. "Mrs. Parker, I'd like you to come in as well." And he hastily marched the protesting lady into his office, Sofia following quickly behind.

"It's all your fault!" Marjorie said, turning to glare at Sofia. Her lips, sans her usual makeup, trembled, and her chin quivered. "I haven't done anything to be dragged in like this. I'm a respectable woman."

Officer Quimby spoke in a calm, authoritative voice. "Mrs. Bennett, we are in the midst of an investigation and merely need to ask you some questions. But you refused to answer the door or respond to our summons."

Marjorie wagged her head back and forth as though denying everything being said.

"Marjorie, I came to talk to you, thinking you might be ill or that something had happened to you," Sofia said, having sufficiently gathered her senses. "But you either weren't home or wouldn't answer the door. I asked the police to check on you, especially when no one at your workplace had heard from you."

"I wasn't hiding. I have a right to my privacy!"

"As do I," Sofia said firmly. "So I must ask you why you told someone at the *Gazette* about my private business. It *was* you who leaked the news about the pouch of gold you saw at my house, wasn't it?"

Marjorie looked up abruptly, then down at her stubby fingers with their gaudy rings. "They put it in the paper?" she asked innocently. "I only told my friend Earline . . . I didn't know. I haven't seen the paper since . . ."

Sofia recalled the neglected papers on the front porch. She was likely telling the truth about not knowing her gossip had been turned into an "About Town" news item. "Well," Sofia said with a heavy sigh, "it's in there for all of Cabot Falls to read, and my family and I are not happy about it."

"The fact is," Officer Quimby broke in, "that pouch of gold has disappeared from the Parkers' home, and that makes it a police matter." He gave Marjorie a penetrating stare. "And because you were there and knew about the gold, you are naturally a suspect."

Marjorie sniffed and looked from Ryan to Sofia with what seemed genuine confusion. "It was stolen?" she asked incredulously. "And you think that I—"

"I ask you again why you have been hiding and refusing to answer your door. If you aren't guilty in this matter—"

"I didn't steal anything!" Marjorie wailed again, rising and tottering on her ridiculous heels. Fresh tears fell down the wrinkled cheeks. "I was hiding because . . . because he's back."

The officer said nothing but gave Sofia a quick glance.

"My ex-husband," she went on. "He's been looking for me, and I didn't want him to find me. I thought if it looked like I'd left town, he'd just go away." She turned to Sofia. "But I'm really sorry about Tiny."

"Tiny?"

"My dog," Marjorie explained. "He's really a lamb."

Sofia gasped. *The monster that almost swallowed us whole is named Tiny?*

"I keep him for protection." Marjorie put her hands out in a helpless gesture. In the silence that followed, she appeared to grow more agitated, and the spots of rouge on her powdered cheeks deepened. She released an exasperated breath. "Well, go ahead, put me in jail! At least I'll be safe from that detestable man!" she cried. "But I say again, I am not a thief!"

"Please sit down, Mrs. Bennett," Ryan said. "No one is calling you a thief." He looked at Sofia with something akin to pleading. He wasn't at his best with hysterical women.

"But Marjorie," Sofia said, "you don't need to hide. If you have good reason to fear your husband—"

"*Ex*-husband," she corrected, sniffing loudly. "And I do. He's a monster."

Whether it was true or not, Sofia couldn't help feeling sorry for her. "You can get a restraining order so he can't come near you." Instinctively, she put an arm around the heaving shoulders. "You do not need to fear this man. Let Officer Quimby help you. There's no need to hunker down inside your house."

Marjorie's face crumpled. "You've always been good to me," she blubbered. "I'm sorry about talking to Earline. You won't turn me out . . ." She sobbed with a fresh paroxysm of weeping. "Out of the painting class, will you?"

Sofia patted Marjorie on the back and rolled her eyes at the young officer over the top of the Georgia O'Keefe wannabe's quivering head.

"I really need coffee," Sofia said when she'd escaped Marjorie Bennett's tearful clutches and was settled into a booth across from Marla. "Thanks for taking a break with me."

Most people thought the head librarian of Cabot Falls was reserved and not inclined to mix. It was true that she was quiet and often serious, but Sofia had quickly found her to be warmhearted and generous. When she'd lost her husband at thirty-eight, it hadn't been easy to raise her son on her own, but Marla was no quitter. And she'd proved herself a shrewd ally to Sofia in working out mysteries connected with the quilt. Now, she clasped her hands on the table and smiled.

"Actually, I have the afternoon off," Marla said. "So I'm in no hurry. I'm all yours . . . if you need me." She signaled the waitress and requested coffee for them both. "And a cheese Danish for me. How about you?"

"A bagel," Sofia answered. "Toasted, with strawberry cream cheese. And a side of bacon—and orange juice." She gave Marla an apologetic look. "I don't think I had any breakfast this morning. At least, I don't remember it. Maybe I'm losing my mind."

Marla leaned in. "Julie told me about the mad dog."

"You mean Tiny," Sofia supplied. Ignoring Marla's incredulous look, she added, "According to Marjorie Bennett, he's gentle as a lamb."

"You found Marjorie?"

"Yes." Sofia let her breath out in a long stream. "Seems she's been hiding out from an ex-husband who suddenly showed up in town. Didn't even put her nose out the door long enough to pick up three days' worth of newspapers."

"So she didn't do it?"

"No. She was shocked to find out the gold was stolen. I'm convinced she had nothing to do with the theft. But she admitted leaking the story of the pouch to a friend who passed it on to the *Gazette*. Suddenly, everyone in town is interested in art or wants me to bake something. Vanessa says boys who never had time for her before are asking her out. Matthew is the center of attention among his playmates. He wants to know when we get the gold back if he can take it to school for show-and-tell. I just wish this would all go away, but we're back to square one. Someone took the pouch Nonna put in that box of drapes. But who?"

"Well, what do we know about that braggart with Bostonian connections who takes art lessons with you? Ernest somebody."

The waitress sidled up to their table. Sofia paused while she served their food.

"Ernest Haynes," Sofia said. "The police are hesitant to delve too deeply into his movements. He's become an upstanding member of the community since moving here. And he supposedly comes from old money. It's hardly likely that he would stoop to take a bag of gold that hasn't even been proved to be real or a nineteenth-century artifact."

"Hmm," Marla mumbled and took another bite of her Danish. "It might be a good idea to check into his background anyway. No one really knows much about him." She paused, probably already considering with her genealogist's brain how to proceed. "What about that new serviceman? You said he was standing on your porch with a clear view into your kitchen window. I wonder how long he's been working for Harvey."

Sofia remembered that she had gone upstairs to get her checkbook to pay for the service call. She'd left him on his own in the basement, and he'd been alone in the kitchen for only a few minutes. Still, it might have been long enough for him to whisk the pouch into his toolbox or pocket. He clearly could have seen the bag from the back porch before she had let him inside. She tried to remember his face and voice. He had very dark hair and brown skin, with an accent that was Mediterranean, or maybe Hispanic.

"I really wasn't worried about leaving him standing in my kitchen while I went for my checkbook," Sofia said thoughtfully. "He looked genuine. His truck displayed the name and logo of the company. It was imprinted on his shirt too, but I didn't know him." She sighed. "I couldn't make out the scrawled signature on the receipt. I thought doctors were the ones who write illegibly."

A twinkle sprang into Marla's quiet blue eyes. "Why don't we pay Harvey a visit? It's just around the corner. And as I said, I have the afternoon off."

Sofia shrugged and drank the last of her coffee. "Guess it wouldn't hurt to talk to him."

Marla was up in a flash, zipping her red hoodie. She never could resist a mystery.

"How can I help you?" asked the receptionist at the heating and cooling establishment when Sofia and Marla arrived. She was a tall, fortysomething woman with big hoop earrings, heavily mascaraed hazel eyes, and a nose that looked as though it had been altered. The nameplate on her jade green suit read Amber.

"Is Harvey around?" Sofia asked.

"Oh, sorry," Amber crooned. She tucked a pen into a mound of overly styled hair and folded her arms across her ample bosom. "Harvey won't be in until tomorrow. Is there something I can do for you?"

"Your serviceman did a furnace check at my house on Saturday. I was just wondering if we might speak with him. You see, a problem has come up—"

"Was there something wrong with his work?" Amber asked, frowning. "We here at Harvey's Heating and Cooling stand behind our work. We want our customers happy."

"No, no. Nothing like that," Sofia responded hastily. "Everything's fine with the furnace. It's just that . . . well, something went missing at my house, and I wondered if your technician might have seen someone in the area when he was, you know, working around the house."

Amber pursed her lips and peered into her computer screen. "Let's see—Saturday." She broke off and drew her penciled brows together. "Um . . . that would be José Martinez, according to the work order here. Is that correct?"

"I believe so," Sofia answered. "Actually, I couldn't read his signature, but he was likely Hispanic—very dark hair, medium height, solidly built."

"This him?" Amber turned the computer screen around to reveal an image of the repairman.

Sofia stepped closer. It was the man who had been at her home. "Yes," she said quietly.

Amber's frown deepened. "I see," she said. "Officer Quimby came looking for him yesterday too. José was out on a call. I gave the officer's card to him when he got back, but—" she put a hand to her lips and drummed them with red-tipped nails "—he called in sick this morning."

"I see," Sofia said, her mind racing with possibilities. *He's left his job and run off, or perhaps he really is sick,* Sofia thought. Avoiding the police made him look very guilty. She locked eyes with Marla and read suspicion in their depths.

Amber frowned. Her mauve-colored lips curled in an expression of distaste. "I told Harvey he shouldn't hire that guy. I told him he would be trouble, and sure enough—"

Marla cut her off. "How long has he been with you?"

"A couple months. Started the first of the year. I told Harvey. I warned him—"

"What's his home address?" Marla asked, clearly annoyed with Amber's rhetoric.

The receptionist drew back, hoop earrings jangling. "I could tell you, but it would get me in trouble. Privacy rules, you know. We have to protect our employees. *Whoever* they are!" Even as she said this, she angled the screen more sharply so the text beneath the photo showed his home address on Union Street.

"Well, thank you for your time," Sofia said. She moved away from the desk, repeating the address in her mind. At the same time, she was unnerved by the receptionist's less-than-professional behavior. "I'll check with Officer Quimby. Perhaps Mr. Martinez will get in touch with him." *If he's got any sense at all, he won't ignore a policeman's request,* she thought. *Unless he's already fled Cabot Falls.*

"Sure sounds like he might be the one who made off with your pouch of gold," Marla said when they were out of earshot. "Amber the receptionist sure thinks so." She paused. "So much for loyalty."

"So much for prejudice." Sofia frowned. "We don't know that the man took anything. There could be a reasonable explanation." She drew in her breath. "We'll get Officer Quimby to follow up on the absent Mr. Martinez. Come back to the house with me.

I'll put the coffeepot on. This has been one crazy Wednesday."

"Sounds good," Marla said.

"Wednesday," Sofia mused when they were on their way. "How does that line go? Something about Wednesday's child being full of woe?"

"Hmm." Marla shook back her shoulder-length hair and cinched her seat belt. "I believe it goes 'Wednesday's child is full of woe, Thursday's child has far to go.' Not sure about Friday or Saturday." She paused to search her librarian's memory. "'Monday's Child' is a fortune-telling song. It's supposed to tell a child's character or future based on the day of birth and to help young children remember the seven days of the week. I believe most days have positive outcomes—except for Wednesday."

"Fits this day," Sofia said. "And we do indeed have a long way to go. If Marjorie Bennett didn't make off with the pouch—and I'm pretty sure she didn't . . ." She paused, remembering how Marjorie had broken down and sobbed on her shoulder. *She's a lonely, sometimes silly, old woman. I can't help but like her.* "I hope she'll be all right."

"Ryan will help her sort out that business with her ex-husband. Imagine hiding out for days, afraid to even go to work!" Marla exclaimed.

Not something Marla could relate to. She was one of the strongest women Sofia knew. It was comforting to have her there as they headed to the Parker home. "But what do we make of José Martinez? Something scared him enough to ignore a police officer's instruction to call and then not show up for work."

"Well, maybe we can make more sense of everything after we put our feet up awhile and have a cup of coffee."

"Sleuthing does wear a person out," Marla said with a wink that meant she was quite happy to expend her energies in pursuit of a mystery.

Sofia turned the corner onto her street. "I wonder what Ryan will make of the fact that Martinez didn't show up for work today," she mused. Suddenly alert, she leaned forward. "Now, what's this all about?"

A police car passed Sophia's Suburban, lights flashing. A group of people milled around a house down at the end of the street. Sofia stared, and her mouth went dry. *My house!*

"Looks like you won't have to call Ryan," Marla said. "There he is now—on your porch. And what's that racket?"

Sofia stared, her stomach doing somersaults. Over the frantic barking of Fergus, she recognized the blaring siren. Her alarm system. Once a month or so, someone in the household forgot to disarm the system before opening a door. The distinctive shrieking that resulted could wake the dead.

She had set the system to instant response before leaving the house that morning. Someone had breached a window or door. Someone had broken in!

10

Mokelumne Hill, California
September 1849

delia followed the sound of breaking crockery to the back of the cook tent, where she had set aside a few biscuits for Quinton. Miners might be willing to pay for home cooking, but someone obviously hadn't been so disposed. The bowl in which she had mixed the bannock had been knocked off the log table and shattered on a large rock.

Turning, she saw a small figure leap toward the woods and disappear from sight.

The figure was small—probably a child. Isaac—Charity and Hannibal Reed's boy? But by this time in the morning, he was usually with his father at the river.

She stood in the morning stillness, more sad than angry, picturing the gangly boy, the small, pinched face and fair hair streaked with dirt. He had a nervous habit of biting his lip, and dark, serious eyes that dwarfed his thin face.

She knew little about Isaac, whom she had witnessed working quietly by his father's side on the trail. He had done his share of carrying water and even hunting with Hannibal, though he couldn't be more than ten years old.

She would gladly have given him a biscuit. He need only have asked. Was he tempted by the aroma of fresh bread and too shy to ask? Hannibal would be incensed. A lay preacher back in his hometown, he placed great stock in principle and the unswerving will of the Almighty.

And what of Charity, remote and absorbed by her loss? Did she even know what her son was feeling? What he was doing? Did Charity offer the tender loving care a mother should give her son? Or was she as solemn and bitter toward him as to everyone else? Anger rose in Adelia's heart.

Charity has lost a child, but what about Isaac, the sad little boy who needs a mother?

Still, it could have been another child who had helped himself to her biscuits. She had only seen the barest glimpse, and the camp was filling up with newcomers. Perhaps they were not all as honorable as the miners she had come to care about. Like Olaf Lundgren, the red-cheeked Swede with one arm shorter than the other who often cut extra firewood to share with her. Or Ezekiel Schmidt, who just that morning had brought a precious cup of fresh milk from his lone surviving cow. He meant it for Quinton and refused to take a pinch of gold in return.

At the rear of her cook tent, she stooped to collect the broken bowl. She rose slowly, holding the shards of earthenware in her hands. It wasn't as though anything truly valuable had been taken. Just a handful of biscuits. Biscuits a miner was willing to pay ten dollars for, though the price was outrageous. She had another bowl, and she could make more biscuits, but what should she do about Isaac Reed or whoever had taken them?

"Is everything all right, Miss Long?"

Startled, she turned to see Wylie Hunter frowning down at her, his dark eyes narrowed in question. He wore an unbuttoned military-style jacket and breeches too fine for the goldfields. Doffing his hat, he smoothed the tousled black hair that dipped to the collar of his shirt.

His horse stood tethered to a tree a few yards away at the edge of the wood. Perhaps he had been visiting the fast-developing rag town of Sacramento again. It was rumored to offer any supplies miners needed as well as entertainments to those who could afford the price.

She stammered a response, unnerved by his closeness and her own accelerated heartbeat. "Yes, I mean . . . there was a . . ." Startled, she felt a shard of the broken crockery cut into her hand. She dropped the offending piece and clutched at her apron to stop the flow.

Wylie stepped closer, eyeing the wound. "You've been hurt." The dark eyes seemed to smolder beneath black brows as he whipped out a handkerchief and quickly pressed it into her hand. "Here, let me help." He patted the cloth, warm from the pocket of his coat, against her wound.

"It is nothing," she protested weakly. "There was someone . . ." She stopped. How could she accuse Isaac or anyone else when she wasn't really sure? And what did three biscuits matter anyway? It was hardly something for Wylie or the "committee" to worry about. Vigilance committees, a means of keeping order, were becoming standard in mining camps, and she wasn't at all sure she trusted them.

"Has someone been troubling you?" he asked, raising an eyebrow and lifting his chin slightly, as though prepared to defend her honor.

What was he doing here? He seemed to spend less and less time panning for gold and more time traveling here and there. Perhaps he had urgent business that she knew nothing about, business that took him away from Mok Hill. He had a way of suddenly appearing at any hour in the camp.

"No. I thought I heard something. I—stumbled and broke my bowl," she said with all the directness she could muster. She gave her head a little toss, aware that she hadn't brushed her hair and that her apron was soiled and untidy. It annoyed her to realize that she cared how she looked in this handsome man's presence. "It's just a tiny scratch," she said gloomily. "Nothing to be concerned about."

He stepped back, leaving the handkerchief in her hand, and surveyed her warily. After a pause, he swept his jacket aside and put a hand to his waist, revealing a handsome leather belt and a holster at his hip. Most of the men carried sidearms, but few so elegantly.

"You should take greater care," he said slowly. He gave a hint of a bow, then, as though he'd nearly forgotten, withdrew something from the inside pocket of his coat. "I picked this up for you while I was getting supplies."

Adelia's heart jumped at the oblong white envelope. A letter! Nothing was more precious, nothing hoped for with more eagerness or yearning. It took many months to receive mail, and everyone in the mining camps was starved for news from home. The post office was just getting going outside of San Francisco. The process of delivering mail was developing from one person carrying letters and packages on a mule to corporations vying for business.

But a letter for her! Her first thought was of Augustus. Dear Augustus, with his poetic soul, his crooked half smile, and eyes the color of a ripening harvest field. The words that had held such promise rang in her mind—words he had spoken with heartbreaking tenderness as he looked into her eyes: *Strange how a moment in your life becomes so important. A whole month or a year can go by, bringing nothing of significance, and then you meet someone . . .*

Had he finally found her? Had he been looking for her all this time and now learned she had gone west with Quinton? She forced herself not to leap forward and snatch the letter from Wylie's hand. Her heart was beating with such force, she wondered if he could hear it.

He was watching her closely with something of a teasing smile. "Since I was picking up a letter at the Sacramento junction, I checked to see if there was anything for Mok Hill, and sure enough, a letter for Miss Adelia Long." He lingered over her name and then pursed his lips as though considering something. "It cost a whole dollar, but I—uh—knew you'd be eager for news."

"How kind of you," she stammered, unable to look away from the letter. Miners often paid dearly for the mail Wylie brought back from Sacramento City and did so willingly. She hoped she had enough to cover this letter. "I will happily pay for your trouble."

"No trouble," he said, cutting her off. "I am honored to be of assistance."

He might be trying to express admiration for her, but she couldn't tell in the wash of delicious expectation. He extended the letter and bowed, this time a bit more deeply, his face retaining that look of humorous inquiry or cunning or something she couldn't identify.

She held the letter flat against her breast and forced herself to wait until Wylie had mounted and ridden away. Then she climbed inside her wagon, propped herself against the roll of quilts, and looked down at the precious thing burning in her hand.

Hope turned to confusion. She had nothing written by Augustus to make a comparison, but this handwriting was familiar and decidedly feminine. She traced her finger over the letters of her name. The writing was clear but slightly wavy. An older person's script. Aunt Felicity.

Adelia felt her heart sink but instantly recover. It would still contain news of home and perhaps of Augustus.

She opened the seal carefully as one might unwrap a treasure. And she read:

> *My dear Adelia,*
>
> *It is my fondest wish that this letter finds you well, wherever you are in the wild western expanse with which our ears are enlightened almost daily. Some of the news we read fills us, I must say, with trepidation and fear for your well-being. And you must know that your uncle and I beseech the Almighty on your behalf and that we wish good fortune for you and Quint.*
>
> *Sadly, I must inform you that my dear mother has been called to her eternal reward following months of confinement to her sickbed. Our small circle of family is bereaved, and I knew you would want to be informed. Your uncle Edward, bless his soul, has been completely supportive and attentive to my own fragile condition. . . .*

Adelia paused in the reading to sigh. Aunt Felicity had complained of her "fragile condition" for as long as Adelia could remember, a condition that never prevented her from participating in the current season's round of soirees.

> *Hiram Powell has married a widow from Chicago— one of the Amos McCathrys whose family owns a chain of very fine hotels. She has not a tenth of your charm, dear girl.*
>
> *As well you know, it could have been you dressed in wedding finery and riding in Hiram's elegant carriage.*

Alas, he couldn't wait for you to accept his proposal. I trust your heart will mend.

Adelia groaned. Her heart would not suffer over the said Mr. Powell, but how she ached for news of someone else. And there was no mention of Augustus Harte. Not one word.

Aunt Felicity commented on the state of mutual family friends and on the rainy June weather that played havoc with her arthritis, ending with a repeated expression of concern for her "dear niece and nephew" who were "out seeking a fortune in the golden West." She signed it with a flourish of swirls around her name, filling out the remainder of the page.

Adelia read the letter over several times, imagining what might have transpired in the months since the letter was written. In spite of her sometimes dread of the fawning Aunt Felicity and the very superior Uncle Edward, it was lovely to hear from home. Lovely to recall familiar places and to think of Papa and Mama and the home they had known together.

I will find a way to post a letter as soon as possible, she decided and refolded the letter and tucked it into her apron pocket. *I will extend my sympathies regarding Mother Parsons and my thanks to Aunt Felicity for her thoughts of me. And I will assure my family that Quint and I are well. But I will not mourn over Augustus. Not for one more moment or one more beat of my heart.*

Yet a small, insistent prayer rose from within her: *Please, let him be all right.*

She sprang from the wagon. It had been too long since she'd checked on Quinton. She'd been sidetracked by the stolen biscuits and Wylie Hunter's appearance with a letter from home. A letter she must share with her brother.

She crept silently into his tent, careful not to disturb him, but he was awake. Blue eyes red rimmed and rheumy from the fever.

A small smile crossed his pale face, and then that look of subtle chagrin she'd seen before. She knew that he hated being sick and unable to work, leaving her to carry on without him.

"Addie . . . I'm sorry . . ."

Adelia's heart lurched. "You've nothing to be sorry about. You couldn't help getting sick, and you're going to get better." She refrained from adding "my poor little man." It would hardly do for an almost twenty-one-year-old who had learned to claw gold out of the earth.

She knelt down to apply a poultice to ease the congestion in his chest. Among her cache of herbs and medicines was Allcock's Porous Plasters, which came highly recommended by a reputable physician in Iowa. She patted the poultice gently against his skin, which felt cooler to the touch than it had a few hours earlier. His breathing seemed less labored too, no longer the frightening rasps that had chilled her heart.

"Yes, you definitely sound better," she said, giving him a wink and another gentle pat.

"You're a good nurse, Addie," he croaked hoarsely. "But I am sorry to cause such trouble—"

"Stop saying silly things," she broke in, "or I'll have to pin your ears to the wall."

His smile widened. "If you think you still can," he remarked weakly and shut his eyes while she smoothed a cool cloth over his forehead. "Maybe tomorrow I can go back to work—at least for a little while."

"You're going to rest and not worry about anything," she said firmly. But without Siba and Hoke, who were working his claim, they would be in real trouble. Competition was strong as more and more gold seekers arrived in California. Long hours often brought small reward. *Our claim is still viable, but how long can the bonanza last?* She deflected her own thoughts, lest Quinton somehow divine them.

"It's all right. Really, it is," she said earnestly. "Siba is as good as his word. He brings the dust back to camp with Hoke every night." Siba took nothing for himself, accepting only the food she sent in a knapsack with Hoke each morning. His race was often exploited because, not knowing what to do with gold, they were willing to work for a plate of stew. Adelia was determined to reserve his wages for him. She would not allow him to be cheated.

"We're going to be fine. I'm so glad to see you looking brighter." She paused, reaching into her satchel. "I brought these along. I thought while you're gaining your strength you might like to use them." She pulled out Quinton's sketch pad and packet of pencils. "You could sit out in the sunshine and sketch some of the scenes of Mok Hill. I bet the men would like to watch. They're always up for entertainment."

Quinton looked first surprised and then dubious, but presently, he traced his finger along one of the drawing sticks.

"And you know what?" she added brightly. "I've learned that the miners are willing to pay for home cooking. There's more than one way to make money."

Quinton raised a blond eyebrow and waited.

"This morning, I was baking biscuits, and a man named John Stoughton gave me ten dollars for some biscuits and promised to buy more tomorrow. I'm going to put out a sign on the cook tent and see who else might be willing to pay for home cooking."

Quinton eased himself up on his pillow. "Poor Addie. I wish I hadn't talked you into this. I shouldn't have dragged you away from Iowa and out into this place where you have to sleep in a wagon and haul water from the creek—" He broke off, coughing from the exertion of speech.

"You didn't drag me anywhere," she affirmed, replacing the dislodged plaster and snugging the quilt closer around him.

"You could have been married by now. You'd be comfortable and well advantaged—"

"And bored to death," she finished. "Besides, no one's asked me yet besides Hiram Powell, and he's already found a marriage partner. One with a sizable dowry." She reached into her apron pocket for the letter. "But I've got a surprise for you."

Quinton pushed himself up higher, blue eyes lighting with anticipation. "It's about time Augustus got around to writing. I bet—" He stopped, seeing something in Adelia's face.

"It's from Aunt Felicity," Adelia stammered, feeling the familiar stab of pain that Augustus's name stirred up. As with almost everything, she had shared with Quinton her admiration of the man who had so quickly stolen her heart and refused to give it back. "Now lie still. I'll read it to you."

The letter brought a smile to Quinton's face, and when the reading was ended, they were both quiet, recalling the old homestead in Iowa where friends called and life moved at a sweet, steady pace. That is, until Papa's business began to fail, along with his health.

Presently, Quinton put his hand over Adelia's, his pale eyebrows knit together. "I'm sorry about Augustus. I wish—"

"I wish you would stop worrying and get some rest," Adelia said with impatience. "I am quite happy as I am, dear brother. I don't need—" She was about to say that she didn't need the likes of Augustus Harte and that she no longer wished to hear his name spoken, but she stopped the words from escaping. "What I need," she said more gently now, "is for you to get well."

She left after convincing him to finish the warm broth she had prepared. It had been a difficult morning, and there was much to do. Water to be brought up from the creek and stored in heavy oaken kegs, food to be prepared, soiled laundry to attend to, and more.

Something had to be done about Isaac Reed. She would have to talk to Charity, a prospect that filled her with both dread and subtle excitement. It would be the first time in months for her to enjoy feminine companionship.

11

Cabot Falls, Vermont
Present Day

"Nothing was taken?" Julie asked in an incredulous whisper from her place across from Marla and Sofia in the Cabot Falls Library.

It was an overcast Thursday morning, the day after Sofia and Marla had discovered the police at the Parker house. Officer Quimby had steered them inside while another officer took down names and addresses of the neighbors who had been looking on.

"Officer Quimby and I checked the house thoroughly, but we couldn't see that anything had even been disturbed," Sofia said. "The alarm on our security system must have scared whoever it was as soon as he—or she—slid the patio door open."

"Do you suppose someone thought there might be more than one bag of gold?" Julie asked, green eyes glinting with excitement.

"Just doesn't make a lot of sense," Marla said, knitting her blond brows together.

"I thought José Martinez might be connected," Sofia said. "He seems to be avoiding Officer Quimby. I expected one of the neighbors to describe a dark-haired man with brown skin fleeing our house. Didn't happen. In fact, no one could say exactly who they saw, just a blurry figure running off."

"Where are nosy neighbors when you need them?" Julie commented with a sigh.

"Well, somebody was after something," Marla said.

"I guess this investigation has opened more than one can of worms," Julie said after a brief silence.

"Yes," Marla said. "Can you believe that receptionist at Harvey's? Accidentally on purpose letting us see Martinez's address?" She had left her desk to huddle with Sofia and Julie but kept her eyes alert to anyone needing her assistance. The three of them were researching some nineteenth-century documents and news reports about the California Gold Rush in hopes of finding references to names in the diary.

Sofia nodded. "I haven't seen such brash bigotry in a while," she said, recalling the curl of Amber's lip and how she had warned Harvey not to hire him. "Adelia Long faced bigotry in California. Last night, I read about how she and her brother befriended an Indian whom the other white miners disliked. Just because he was a Native American. His name was Siba, a Cahuilla who was educated by Spanish missionaries. He became quite a protector for Adelia and worked their claim with Quinton Long."

Marla handed Sofia a computer printout. "I found this article about Native Americans during the Gold Rush." She leaned over Sofia's shoulder and read, "'The huge numbers of newcomers drove them from their traditional hunting, fishing, and food-gathering areas. To protect their homes and livelihood, some of them responded by attacking the miners.'" She shook her head before continuing. "'Of course, this provoked counterattacks on native villages. The Native Americans, outgunned, were often slaughtered. Some 4,500 California Indians were killed between 1849 and 1870, while many more perished due to diseases brought in.'"

"Adelia went west at the very beginning of the rush," Sofia said. "She said many of them feared attack by Native Americans.

But this seldom happened. Instead, the forty-niners fell victim to cholera, mountain fever, pneumonia, and diphtheria." She paused, recalling what she had read so far in the diary. "Adelia was quite knowledgeable about herbs and medicines. She nursed the sick in the camps and on the trail. No wonder the miners looked up to her."

Julie broke in. "That diary is priceless, Sofia. And to think the pouch your grandmother left might actually have come from California in 1849. We've got to find it—and protect it." Her characteristic fire was heating up. "Tell me how I can help."

"I wish I had been more observant," Sofia lamented. "There was just so much going on at the house the day the pouch disappeared."

"There's always so much going on at your house," Marla said. "I'm not sure how you could expect to keep track of it all."

"I guess there will be one less distraction. I've lost an art student," Sofia said glumly. "And I was counting on his fee."

"Mr. Haynes?" Marla asked.

Sofia lowered her head. He had been pretty incensed when he had terminated his association with her art class. He had phoned in the midst of dinner the night before.

"Mom, it's for you," Luke had called from the hallway.

"Why must people call at the dinner hour?" Jim had groused. But he had immediately given her a fond smile. He knew how upset she was about the loss of the pouch and especially the feared loss of her sisters' esteem. They'd been pretty hard on her for not safeguarding such an important artifact.

She had taken the receiver, quickly moving it several inches from her ear as defense against the angry blast that followed.

"This is Ernest Haynes, and I wish to advise you that I will not be attending your art classes in the future." His fricative words stung the air. "I will not be patronizing your substandard studio after you had the police haul me in for questioning.

Accusing me like a common criminal! I'll have you know my family is one of the most elite in Boston—or anywhere, for that matter. And we do not suffer fools gladly."

It was over the top. Ludicrous. She had been treated to the man's ego before and always tempered her responses. She apologized for his trouble but affirmed that the police were checking with everyone involved. It was just routine, and she had meant no offense. Far from mollified, however, he had simply ranted on about the good name of his family that she had carelessly besmirched.

"You may ship my personal art supplies as well as any of my paintings to my address," he had said after her apology.

This was too much for Sofia. "I'm sorry," she had said, struggling to keep her voice even, "but I do not believe your personal items are my concern, but you are welcome to come and get them. Do call for a convenient time." And she had hung up before he could retort.

Marla and Julie were waiting for her to come back to the moment, to confirm the identity of the lost art student. She shook herself from her reverie. "Yes, it was Ernest. He's dropped the class. His pride was hurt, and we all know he has plenty of that commodity. Can you believe he actually ordered me to ship his paint supplies and paintings to his address?"

"Why, that pompous banty rooster!" Julie fumed. "You didn't do it, did you?"

"No. I'm afraid he really got my dander up though." She let her breath out slowly. "At least Marjorie wants to continue her lessons. Actually, she begged me not to drop her."

"Hopefully it wasn't because she wants to be within snooping distance," Julie said, raising a ginger-colored eyebrow.

The Pinot Painters waded through more articles and references before Julie announced that she had shopping to do. Marla had to get back to her desk as the library began filling up. She gave Sofia a hug, which was special because Marla wasn't usually demonstrative. "We'll get to the bottom of this," she said quietly.

"Yes," Julie chimed in with her ready encouragement. "Officer Quimby is no slouch. He's probably caught up to Mr. Martinez by now."

Sofia paused as the address for José Martinez repeated itself in bold numerals in her mind—211 Union Street. It was a ways across town, but she just might have time to check it out. Maybe she could go by the house and see if there were any signs of life. *What would it hurt just to drive by?*

You won't do anything rash, will you? That had been Jim's warning before he'd headed off to school that morning. *Just let the police handle this.*

The afternoon air was mild with the promise of spring. No rain was expected, but an overcast sky added to her mild gloom as she headed toward the south of Cabot Falls. It was less picturesque than some parts of town, the houses older and a few needing repair. But most residents appeared to take pride in their property, adding to the genuine charm that brought many tourists to the area in summer and fall. At any time of the year, the majestic peaks of surrounding mountains cradled verdant valleys, and there was no shortage of sparkling lakes and creeks for fishing, swimming, or simply enjoying.

As she drove along a main artery that led to Union Street, she spotted a car wash. It had been days, weeks maybe, since she'd taken the time to spruce up the Suburban. Jim liked to wash the cars himself, but since his illness, she had tried to spare his energy. She pulled into the queue and went inside to pay for the service and to wait while the automatic brushes and tubes whirred. Once the SUV came out, someone would sluice off the water with a squeegee and wipe it down.

While she waited, she pondered just how to approach José Martinez—that was, if she could find him. He'd certainly had opportunity to tuck away the bag of gold while she was upstairs finding her checkbook. She practiced a few opening lines as she watched the progress of her car through the line. None seemed reasonable. She was beginning to think this wasn't a good idea when suddenly she caught sight of something that made her breath stop. Not something, but someone.

Did that dark-skinned man wiping down a late-model Honda just *look* like José Martinez? She stared at him as he bent to the work, his straight black hair falling into his eyes. Dark, heavily lashed eyes, eyes she remembered.

What was he doing washing cars? He'd called in at Harvey's Heating and Cooling to say he was sick, but here he was, working in a car wash. She stood rooted to the spot. The other man working with Martinez wiped the inside of her car's door and left it open, signifying that it was ready for her. She hesitated. If she came out now, Martinez was likely to recognize her. She could hardly engage him in a serious conversation while he was working.

But Martinez moved away and began washing the vehicle behind hers. She pulled up the collar of her coat and slipped out to retrieve her car, nodding to the man who stood by her door. Martinez hadn't seen her. She drove out onto the street, feeling her pulse race.

He called in sick yesterday and obviously didn't go in to Harvey's today, but he's washing cars. Harvey couldn't have fired him—not yet. Harvey wasn't even in the office on Wednesday. Totally puzzled, Sofia kept going, her GPS indicating that Union Street was one mile ahead.

She turned onto Union thinking she'd just have a look at the house. Or maybe she could park a little ways from 211 and wait in the car for Martinez to appear. Or turn around and go home, report to Ryan Quimby. Let him handle it. Jim would like that.

She drove slowly past 211, a low-rise bungalow with a front porch. The gunmetal shingles would probably benefit from a coat of paint. A second story had been added, built into a sloping roof with dormer windows. Grass was sparse around the house, but a low boxwood hedge lined one side. She saw no one about, but a tricycle had been left abandoned at the foot of the porch steps.

She drove around the block and surveyed the house again. She was still arguing with herself about what to do when a young woman stepped onto the porch, holding a baby on her hip. She wore jeans, a loose-fitting top, and a red scarf tied around curly black hair. _José's wife?_ Sofia watched the woman pick something up and quickly return inside.

Sofia parked outside the bungalow and walked up to the door. Taking a deep breath to calm herself, she prayed for the right words.

The baby still perched on her hip, the woman opened the door and stared out with a puzzled expression. Her eyes were large, quite beautiful, and decidedly frightened.

"Please," Sofia began, "I'm sorry to trouble you, but I know your husband. He, uh, serviced our furnace last week." She paused and tried a smile. "He did an excellent job. May I come in? Just for a moment?"

"José is not home. He is at work," she said in a decided Hispanic accent.

Sofia felt sorry for her obvious discomfort. She wondered if the woman knew that her husband was working at a car wash instead of Harvey's Heating and Cooling. "Perhaps I could wait? My name is Sofia. Sofia Parker."

"I am Melina Martinez, but I . . ."

A high-pitched wail suddenly erupted, followed by anguished crying that sounded like a toddler in distress. Melina turned with a gasp as a little boy not more than three clambered in, holding his right hand up in the air. A trickle of blood rushed from his index finger. "Mama!" he cried over and over as his mother rushed toward him. A girl with a runny nose watched wide-eyed from the hallway. Likely she had been too sick to attend school.

"Let me hold the baby for you," Sofia said, reaching for the infant girl, thus allowing her mother to comfort the little boy. "Hush, it's all right," she cooed to the chubby-faced bundle in her arms. It had been a long time since her children had been this small.

"Please, sit down," Melina told Sofia over her shoulder as she gathered her little boy in her arms. She inspected the toddler's wound, murmuring something in Spanish. Mother language that needed no translation.

The living room was comfortably cluttered but clean. A blanket had been placed over the worn couch on which Sofia planted herself with the pudgy baby in her arms. She stared at her for a few seconds and then broke out in a toothless grin that touched Sofia. "She's a sweetheart," she said over the toddler's gradually diminishing wails.

When quiet was restored, Melina Martinez sat down on a blue-and-white-flowered chair. "Gracias," she said, nodding toward her baby, who continued to grin and play with the tie on Sofia's hoodie. She looked up with puzzled eyes. "Why do you want to see my husband?"

Before Sofia could answer, José himself stepped through the front door, which had been left ajar. He put his hand on the door-frame and stared at the scene in his living room. He looked tired. Sweat rings marked his soiled blue shirt. He closed the door and brushed damp hair from his forehead, wary eyes trained on Sofia.

"Mrs. Parker? Is everything okay—with your furnace?"

"Oh," Sofia said, rising and handing the baby back to her mother. "My furnace is working fine, but—" She floundered, wondering how to proceed. The man seemed genuinely confused to see her. "Your work was fine," she repeated, then hesitated again before blurting out, "Mr. Martinez, do you know that Officer Quimby has been looking for you? I also went to your company and asked to see you. I was told you were ill."

He appeared startled, and Sofia wondered if he might bolt from the house. She continued quickly.

"The police are investigating a theft that occurred the day of your service call. Mr. Martinez . . ." She hesitated. "You see, something quite valuable was taken from my house. No one is saying you did it, but you were there. The police are questioning everyone who came to my house last Saturday."

José rubbed a work-worn hand over his jaw and shook his head as though to wake from a bad dream. "I—I did not know. I thought—" He tried again. "I did not take anything. I swear I did not."

"But you ignored the police and you did not go to work after he came to find you." She tried to read his face. It was a good face that didn't appear to hold any deceit. But who knew what lay behind another's eyes?

"I thought the police would bring trouble—with my visa," he said. "I was afraid." He lowered his head and passed his hand over his jaw again.

"Do you mean you aren't registered to work in this country?" Sofia asked.

"No. I am, but there has been some trouble with my green card. I have been trying to straighten it out. But the police—when they came, I was afraid. I don't want to go back to Guatemala and leave my family." He dropped down on the couch and held his head in his hands. "And now you think I have stolen something—"

"I am not accusing you. Please understand. The police must talk to everyone about it. I'm sorry for your visa trouble. But surely if you are honest, the police will work with you to sort it out." Sofia paused. "I saw you today at the car wash. I don't understand. You're a trained technician."

"I have to feed my family," he said softly. He lowered his head and was quiet for a long moment. "It costs a lot of money to pay the lawyer. I wash cars on my off hours to fill in."

"But you can't just stay away from your work with Mr. Harvey," Sofia said.

"I am afraid he will fire me." José's fists clenched at his side.

"If you don't show up for work, he will for sure," Sofia said.

Melina and José both looked like they could break down weeping any second, and Sofia's heart ached for them. Here was a man trying to take care of his wife and children and to work out the complicated machinations of immigration.

Sofia left, feeling certain—or almost certain—that she could cross José Martinez off her list of suspects. She sighed. *But where do I go from here?*

12

Mokelumne Hill, California
October 1849

*D*owsing the last embers of the campfire, Adelia went in search of Charity Reed, whose site lay about a half mile from hers. A chill in the morning air warned that, though October remained mild, winter was crouched in the mountains surrounding Mok Hill. In that part of California, winter meant rain—sometimes drenching, bone-chilling, torrential rains.

Miners were putting up rude buildings constructed from just about any available material to keep the dampness out. Herman Kaufman's house was a room about twenty feet square, lined over the top with stitched-together cotton cloth that stretched apart in many places so that the shingles above were visible. The sides were hung with fabric and the fireplace was built of stones and mud. A beam of wood covered with strips of tin from cans formed the mantel. Many of the cans still bore the names of the eatables they formerly contained. A hole cut in one side of the room made a two-foot-square window.

Adelia knew it was of particular distress to Quinton that he was unable to provide a proper shelter for her. "I promised you a cabin before winter, and here I lie, a useless heap."

She had tried to reassure him that there was plenty of time. "Soft breezes and bright sunshine yet bless our days, and we've plenty of quilts and fire for warmth."

But now, as she drew her shawl more tightly across her shoulders, she wondered just how long it would be before the winter rains descended—and what that would mean for them all.

It would be nothing like the midwestern winters in Iowa. She recalled days when snow poured from heaven's relentless sieve, dressing fields in thick, white drapery and causing the line between land and sky to disappear. Roads became impassable. Everyone hunkered down inside their homes before a perpetual fire.

Melancholy overwhelmed her as she thought about their last winter before Papa died. It had been a particularly cold season. Deep cold. And perhaps because of the conditions, everyone had made a special effort at cheer. Lamps were trimmed more brightly, music rang with lively enthusiasm and frequency, and guests stayed for long, luxurious periods as they waited for roads to become passable.

These thoughts, added to Quinton's comments about Augustus, brought memories of that last Christmas Eve. A three-day storm had ended, leaving the Iowa countryside beneath a glistening blanket of snow several feet deep. The moon shone down on the hills with a brightness that rivaled day, and everyone felt the hush and glory of it. Augustus had gotten special leave from his post and reached their home by a borrowed one-horse sleigh.

I said I would give him no further thought, she told herself as she walked. *But here I am, drawing him back to me with such sweet pleasure.*

He could stay only a few hours, she recalled, but those hours were filled with such delight that even now she was breathless with the joy of it. They had sat together long after Papa and Quinton and Adelia's two cousins had retired. They sipped hot cider by the fire and roasted chestnuts on long spears, crunching the sweet delicacies. In her mind's eye, she could see the red tinge on Augustus's slightly oversize ears as the fire grew hotter. Straw-colored hair dipped over his forehead when he bent to place the skewer into the fire.

"I am grieved that I have no gift for you," Augustus had said before they parted for what would be the last time. And indeed, she had none for him, his visit coming as a total surprise. Yet they had no need of mementos.

"Your visit is gift enough," she had said shyly, knowing with what difficulty he must have driven the horse over many snowy miles to reach her. She knew as well that Augustus earned little. Military pay was paltry, hardly enough to hold body and soul together. But then, times were hard for them all.

"Someday," he had said with fierce longing and hope, "I will build something of value. I will do something worthy of life and living." He paused, looking away. "I have no special talent . . . like your gift of aiding the sick. I'm but a poor farmer, and an even poorer soldier."

Nothing tied Augustus to the Minnesota town that had been his home as a child. Both parents were killed in an accident on their small farm. His only sister had perished in a cholera epidemic that had ravaged the area. No home fires burned for him. It was no wonder he had signed up with the closest regiment and gone off to war. Surely it was a worthy thing to fight for one's country, but it had proved heartache for her.

"I can't thank you enough for sharing these few hours with me, my dear Miss Long. Your house is full of warmth and kindness. It spreads to everyone fortunate enough to call. For me, Christmas is often hard to bear, remembering."

He had turned his face to the fire, probably to hide the sadness etched in it.

At that moment, she had longed to touch his hand, to dispel the sorrow so evident in his expression, but she had not. They were as yet "Miss Long" and "Mr. Harte" to each other. It was a formality that might well be thought ludicrous in the casual culture of the fast-expanding West. The rugged frontier life seemed to take the nonsense out of people, teaching practical wisdom and rare judgment of men. Her reverie, only briefly interrupted, continued.

"But it is wrong to harbor grief in the soul at this time when such joy entered our world," Augustus had added as the fire crackled in the grate. "It's Christmas, and I repent of my careless words in the face of sacred bounty."

Few farmers, in Iowa or anywhere, spoke with such lyricism and depth. His admitted early love of books had often earned him a scolding as a boy, he had told her during that memorable Kanesville dance. Instead of mucking out the stable, he had climbed into the hayloft and "traveled the world of wonder and adventure."

Oh, Augustus! Had he been among the casualties of war? A war that claimed seventeen thousand lives and wounded many more? Had he succumbed to some dread sickness that no skill of hers could heal? Or had he simply forgotten her?

Adelia's heart plummeted. She wanted to be angry, to dismiss him as insensitive, arrogant, or worse. But if he was dead—or at least dead to her—why did some inner fire continue to smolder in her heart? Why could she not let go and get on with her life?

Her life on her trek west, in spite of the struggle and hardness, had given her opportunity to bring comfort to the sick and help Quinton secure sufficient capital to begin fresh back home. She had found life in California immensely freeing, at times even exhilarating. And they were surrounded by a beauty she hadn't known existed.

She paused to admire a view of the amazing Sierras turning

golden in the sunlight. In the evenings, they took on a rich purple hue that left her breathless.

Adelia sighed. *Yes, this is a wild, untamed country, but it's one in which a woman as well as a man can prove what she is made of. Perhaps I, too, can do something worthy,* she thought, echoing Augustus's words.

That, for the moment, involved a former dance hall girl and a young boy who had stolen three biscuits from her cook tent. When the Reeds' wagon came into view, Adelia approached, refusing to let her fear of a confrontation deter her. Charity was Isaac's mother, and she needed to know if her son was taking a wrong turn that might lead to a worse offense.

She frowned at the clutter of tools, crockery, cans, and clothing that bulged out beneath the Reeds' wagon. The ground under a wagon was often used to store implements and household necessities that needed to be protected from dampness, animals, or pests. Keeping these things in an orderly fashion was not an easy task, and it appeared that the Reeds found it challenging.

Suddenly, she stopped, hearing the strains of a feminine voice in a sad, raspy lament. A woman singing was rare in the world of bearded men in boots, flannel shirts, and trousers saturated with muck of bar or hillside. She waited, trying to catch the words.

"Hush, hush," she heard in a small strangled voice. She stepped closer and peered through a small opening in the osnaburg.

Charity Reed was dressed in a colorless cotton gown and sitting up among a clutter of bedclothes. Tangled hair fell over her thin shoulders like a black waterfall, and brown eyes flecked with gold appeared too large for the narrow oval of her face. She held something in her lap and stared down at it as her lips moved.

"Hush, hush, time to be sleeping. Hush, hush, dreams come a-creeping." The voice, soft and lyrical, was heavy with sadness. "Dreams of peace and of freedom. So smile in your sleep, bonny baby. Hush, hush."

She sang the words over, moving her head from side to side in accompanying rhythm. She seemed transported, rendering her face almost pretty. "So smile in your sleep, bonny baby. Hush." She broke off suddenly, lifted deeply shadowed dark eyes, and caught Adelia's gaze.

"Hello, Mrs. Reed," Adelia called brightly. She held up a bottle that contained a mixture of brewer's yeast and honey, a drink known to soothe sore throats such as Charity had suffered from during the overland journey. Now, however, she seemed recovered, able even to sing. Yet she had avoided their company at the evening campfires and earned a reputation for brooding and silence. "I brought you something."

"Go away!" she cried with small, quick shakes of her head like a petulant child. She pursed her lips in a pout. The strap of her gown fell away, revealing a thin white shoulder, which made her appear all the more vulnerable inside the shadowy wagon.

"Please. I came to see if you're all right. I'm Adelia Long. We met on the train when your child was sick. Remember?"

Charity stopped swaying and knit her black brows together. "My child?" she repeated in a dreamy singsong. She looked down into her lap once more, and Adelia saw she was holding a small gilded frame with a daguerreotype inside. It had to be the daughter she had lost, the child to whom she was singing. Had Charity become unhinged? If so, she wouldn't be the first to be overcome by the rigors of an eighteen-hundred-mile trek across bleak desert and forlorn plain.

This is definitely outside my small expertise with herbs and medicines, Adelia thought, feeling a chill come over her. "Please, may I come in?" she persisted, grabbing a toehold and hoisting herself up on the wagon's wooden platform.

"My child?" Charity asked again, seeming not to notice that Adelia was inside and approaching the bed where she sat. "My baby?" She cocked her head to one side, gave Adelia a vacant smile, and held the frame toward her. "This is my baby," she said. "She's sleeping now." After a few seconds, she shrugged and withdrew her arm. She dropped the frame upside down beside her on the blanket.

"But I meant—"

"No," Charity said, interrupting. She crossed her arms and looked up at Adelia, clarity registering in her eyes. "Actually, my baby isn't sleeping." Her lips twisted in irony. "She's dead."

"I know," Adelia said softly. "And I'm very sorry. But I meant your other child—Isaac. I'm glad to see he is well and able to help his father at the diggings." She looked around the untidy interior of the wagon and drew her breath in sharply. On a wooden barrel next to the bed were three round biscuits, the biscuits she had baked that morning. The pitifully thin Charity had taken only a small bite from one.

What should I do now? Adelia contemplated. But suddenly the wagon flap opened and Isaac stepped in, eyes wide. He looked from Adelia to his mother and back again, clearly frightened. Adelia could see the boy's pulse throbbing in his neck. His face appeared ashen, even though he was well tanned from sun and wind. Adelia heard herself say, "Hello, Isaac. It was very thoughtful of you to bring your mother the biscuits I gave you. I'm sure she will find them nourishing."

The boy set down a flask of water by the bed and gave his mother a look of such eager tenderness that Adelia felt like an intruder. She pondered the boy. He had stolen, not for himself, but for the love of his mother. He must be called to account for it, but not now, not in front of Charity. She smoothed a spot on her apron and smiled at Isaac. "Stop by my wagon tomorrow morning, and I'll give you some fresh ones to bring your mother. Okay?"

Isaac gave her a half nod, eyes averted, clearly bewildered, and quickly jumped down to the ground and fled.

Adelia turned to Charity. "That boy dearly loves you. I believe he'd do just about anything for you. So would Hannibal."

Charity swayed slightly and pressed her lips together. After a few seconds of silence, she turned the daguerreotype around again and traced her finger over the tiny face, the soft curls. "Hannah was just beginning to smile, and when she nursed, she liked to hold my finger. Sometimes she stroked it softly—so softly."

Adelia swallowed against a lump in her throat. She didn't know what it was to love a baby, but she knew what it was to lose someone dear.

"She took the fever and got sicker and sicker, and then she was gone. Hannibal says it was God's will." The dreamy quality returned to Charity's voice. After a few seconds, she spoke again. "Why did God take my baby when we loved her so?"

Adelia reached for Charity's hand and held it gently in both of hers. She waited until their gazes caught and held. "God didn't take your baby," she said softly but with conviction. "Death took her, but God accepted her, and she's safe in His arms. She is loved more than we can ever imagine." Adelia smiled at the grief-stricken woman. "And one day you'll see her again."

The brown, almond-shaped eyes closed briefly and returned to Adelia's face. She searched it silently for a long moment before looking away. "Why have you come?" She was perfectly lucid now.

Adelia wasn't sure how to answer. She'd come to report Isaac's theft, to express her disapproval of Charity's disregard and her unneighborly attitude toward all the miners. But she hadn't been prepared for the woman's desperate pain.

"Because we're a family here. We need to take care of one another." She smiled. "I would very much like to be your friend, Charity Reed."

"I can't see why," Charity said grimly after a long silence. I've been nothing but a burden to everyone." She shook her head. "Especially to my husband. And I've been a terrible mother to Isaac."

"You've been ill, Charity, and your heart is broken. It's time to let it heal. Your boy needs you. He needs to know you love him."

Charity nodded slowly, took a deep breath, and let it out in a sigh. "It's good of you to come. I needed to talk to someone." She brushed back a strand of unruly hair. "I look a fright, I know, and I haven't been a hostess by any measure." She indicated the less-than-tidy interior of her wagon. "I haven't even offered you a cup of coffee."

"It's nothing that can't be righted," Adelia said, feeling a rising in her soul. "Do you feel strong enough for a little walk? The air is beautiful this time of day. I haven't had anyone to talk to about—you know—things a woman wants to talk about." She grinned, seeing understanding in Charity's eyes. "Have you ever seen such a collection of grubby old men as we have here?"

The sun had chased away the chill of morning as the two walked past tent sites and the fenced meadow where animals grazed. They talked about their families and their hopes for the future. Adelia was surprised how quickly they became easy with each other and how pleasant Charity could be when her mind wasn't burdened with her private pain.

"My brother has been ill, but I found him much improved this morning," Adelia said. "He's eager to get back to his claim, but I hope I can convince him to wait awhile."

"It's hard to make men wait when there's so much gold wanting to be plucked up," Charity said, pausing to take a breath and leaning against a tree.

"We've been a busy, happy community," Adelia noted, "but as competition grows, I fear for the tempers of miners. Yesterday, Peter Hansen got into a scuffle with his partner, but I think the culprit was the whiskey they brought back from a saloon in Rich Bar." She sighed, wishing it wasn't so easy for men to fall into temptation, to spend their money on worthless pursuits.

They walked in silence for a while. Most of the miners were gone to the diggings, but a few took the morning sun outside their tents or shanties. Adelia saw that two new privies had been erected on a grassy slope away from the double row of dwellings. They walked along the makeshift road that was well tamped down by wheels, hooves, and human feet.

"Look how many more tents and wagons have joined us," Adelia commented.

"You're right. Before long, we'll be a booming town."

"You should rest now," Adelia said, noting Charity's accelerated breathing. "I think we should head back to your wagon." She took Charity's slender arm, pleased that she did not draw away.

They were walking companionably, enjoying the rich sunshine on their backs, when suddenly a man came tearing out of a tent a hundred yards up the slope. He yelled something indistinguishable, flailed his arms, and stomped his boots.

Adelia halted, arm in arm with Charity, and stared at a man with bushy red hair sticking out from a dingy slouch hat. He had an equally bushy beard and a round, red face. Calvin Means, a rough old prospector with a raucous laugh who liked to regale anyone who would listen with tall tales from his travels. But he wasn't laughing now, and what he said made Adelia's heart sink.

"That there bag was plumb near filled!" he roared, drawing a small crowd around him. "Ain't but a pittance left. I've been robbed!" He shook his meaty fists in the air, and his beard trembled with rage. "Done took my watch too!" And then the big man began to sob drunkenly. "He stole my daddy's watch."

13

Cabot Falls, Vermont
Present Day

The morning after her confrontation with José Martinez, Sofia sat across from Jim in their comfortably cluttered kitchen. With the children gone and Jim not needing to be in class until nine, the two of them were enjoying coffee together. "You should have seen them," Sofia began, taking a sip of steaming coffee. "Mr. Martinez and his family, I mean."

"You promised not to do anything rash," Jim said, narrowing perceptive blue eyes.

"I didn't promise," she said. "And it wasn't rash. I just went by his house to see if he was there. I mean, when he didn't show up for work after Ryan's visit—"

"You couldn't leave it to the police, could you?" There was no anger in his voice. Just concern tinged with knowing humor. "I guess you didn't actually promise, but it could have been dangerous."

She nodded, touched by the tenderness in his voice. *How fortunate I am to have such a good and understanding husband,* she thought. She didn't want to cause him anxiety, but her penchant for the mysterious was something she couldn't deny.

She recounted her experience entertaining the Martinez baby while Melina tended to the toddler's accident. "They are so young and trying to make their way in a new country. It can't be easy, especially with all those children." She thought about the anguish she'd seen on their faces when she told them about the purpose of the police visit. She'd tried to read guilt there but found only openmouthed surprise. Surely José had not been the one to make off with her property.

"What do you think will happen to them?" Jim asked, concern etched in his features. "Immigration officials are cracking down on illegals."

"He insists he isn't an illegal alien. He's registered to work here, but there's some problem with his visa, and he's into an immigration lawyer for big bucks. I hope Harvey will help him. I'd hate to see a trained furnace repairman consigned to washing cars to feed his family." She sighed. "But we're still in the dark about what happened and why someone wanted to break into our house."

Jim got up from his chair and walked around to stand behind Sofia. Leaning down, he placed both arms around her shoulders. "And you, my little Agatha Christie, will not rest until you solve this puzzle, will you?" He kissed the top of her head. "I wish you were going with us to Matthew's basketball game tonight."

"I hate to miss it this time, but I've got to finish another order of coconut macaroons. Heather needs them in the morning—all eight dozen. But dinner will be early, so you'll have plenty of time to get to the game." Sofia gave his hand a lingering clasp before he headed out with his briefcase. "Love you," she called after him.

And she did—fiercely and deeply. Throughout their years together, she had never regretted saying yes. She remembered how he had knelt on one knee to propose, lost his balance, and rolled onto his side. They had both collapsed in laughter that in seconds had turned into a passionate embrace.

"My football knee plays jokes on me at the worst times," he

had said when their long kiss was ended. "But will you?"

"Will I what?" she couldn't help but ask innocently.

"Marry me and make me the happiest person on earth?"

"Can't," she had responded in all seriousness. "I can never make you the happiest person on earth, because that's what I am—with you."

Had Adelia Long felt such love for Augustus Harte? Adelia believed he had abandoned her, but she hadn't been able to cast him from her heart. Sofia picked up the diary she had brought down when she came to breakfast.

> *At night, when the campfire flickers and my heart yearns for home, Augustus intrudes. I see his eyes the color of ripening wheat. I hear again his words: 'You, Miss Long, are never but a short step from my heart.' Dear Augustus, with his poetic soul, his crooked half-smile. He made me believe I was more important to him than anything in the world.*

> *Wherever he is and whatever has happened to him, he clearly has no interest in me now. I am tortured to imagine his warm amber eyes turned toward a delicate wife and rosy-cheeked children.*

After months with no word, Augustus had ridden up to Mok Hill looking for her.

> *I braced myself against the tent pole and blinked to be sure I wasn't dreaming. Could it be Augustus—my Gus? For so I had secretly named him in my heart. He stood now before me, handsome, sun-browned, wearing a dapper suit and shiny boots, and looking like the wealthy*

merchant he no doubt was. But my heart grew hard. Surely in all this time he might have found some way to contact me, if he cared at all.

Augustus had explained his absence, his longing to have something to offer the woman he loved. He did love her. Sofia felt sure of this. And from the many recollections Adelia had put into her diary, Sofia was sure Adelia had loved him.

"They must not let each other go," she said in a whisper to the empty kitchen. Especially since that self-styled vigilante Wylie Hunter was waiting in the wings to woo her—or to fool her. It was hard to tell from what Adelia wrote so cryptically.

It annoys me to realize that I care how I look in this handsome man's presence, for I fear something in Wylie Hunter's dark personality, the hidden rumble of his anger. Troubling rumors about his less-than-wholesome activities have arisen. And he will be rid of Siba if he has his way.

Sofia moved closer to the window with the diary. She stared thoughtfully through the glass, wondering about what she had learned through documents related to California's Gold Rush. With Marla's and Julie's help, she'd found some connections to people Adelia described. A reference to Hoke Adams indicated that after leaving the goldfields, he had married a seamstress and opened a dry goods store in Arizona in 1855. The prospector had turned retailer. By all accounts in Adelia's journal, he must have been an upright, if colorful, one.

Quinton Long had taken his modest earnings from the goldfields and had gone to art school, where he met his wife. By 1880, he was a father of two and was teaching at a university in Iowa City.

Siba's trail had gone quickly cold. Sofia wished she could have known the young Cahuilla brave who had faithfully watched over Adelia, saving her life from a dangerous snake and working Quinton's claim while he was ill.

Sofia picked up her coffee and continued to stare out the window. A few cars went by, but one remained idling not far from the school bus stop. A late-model sedan, dark blue or black, with a clear view of the Parker house. She put down her coffee again and sat up straight, suddenly alert. It was the same car she'd seen when she had watched Matthew walk to the stop and get on the bus nearly a half hour earlier. Sometimes parents waited along that stretch until their children had safely boarded the bus. But why was the dark sedan still there? She recognized most of the neighbors' vehicles. This one was new to her. Was someone watching their house? There had been one attempt at a break-in. Why not another?

Then, as though divining that it was the object of scrutiny, the car moved off at a moderate pace and disappeared.

Am I getting paranoid? Possibly, but if that car comes back, I'm calling Ryan Quimby. She remained at the window—five minutes, maybe ten—but the car did not reappear.

"I'm losing it," Sofia said aloud with a hollow laugh, and she reached for her cup of coffee. It had gone cold—stone cold. She put it down in distaste. Time to stifle a far-too-active imagination and get on with the day. She set about clearing the table but couldn't help glancing out the window from time to time. But the dark sedan did not reappear. *Get a grip, Sofia Parker,* she told herself. But when the phone rang suddenly, she jumped all the same.

"That you, Sofia? You sound strange." Marla's cultured voice broke through her reverie.

"Sorry. I was just, um, thinking about all that's happened.

You know, going over the clues—or lack thereof." Sofia warmed to her good friend's voice. "What's up? You at the library?"

"Where else? But listen, Sofia. I found something interesting."

Marla was helping her look for information on all the suspects in the case of the missing pouch. She was a formidable cybersnoop and seldom left any virtual stone unturned. "Really? I could use some good news about now."

"Everything okay?"

"Fine," Sofia assured her. "What do you have?"

"I found something about that Wylie Hunter from your diary. It may be nothing pertinent to the missing pouch, but it's worth pursuing. I don't think we should discuss it on the phone. Library's pretty quiet today, but I can't get away. Can you come by?"

"You sound very mysterious," Sofia said.

"I can't talk now. I have customers." She paused, and Sofia heard her give someone the location of a book. "Come around eleven, if you can. Bring a Cinnamon Dolce Light from our favorite coffee shop."

Sofia hung up. What Marla found was probably interesting, but would it yield any clues about Nonna's odd bequest? Still, she was intrigued. Though she had a great deal to do, she'd meet Marla at the library. Good thing she had planned to stay home this evening. With everyone gone, she could whip out that new order of macaroons pretty quickly once she bought the supplies.

She put a small pork roast, along with potatoes and carrots, in the slow cooker. With dinner on and Matthew's jersey churning in the dryer, she could head off to the library. By way of the coffee shop, of course. Being with Marla always cheered her. *Strange how a friend's call can change your outlook.* She picked up Nonna's diary from the table and tucked it inside the bread box. *As good a hiding place as any for now,* she thought and slid it under the loaf of bread.

She armed the security system, closed the door, and slid behind the wheel, hoping her umbrella was in the backseat, for the weather had taken a turn. Dark clouds were moving low and rapidly across the sky, and a blustery wind whipped greening trees. *So much for my clean car,* she thought, turning onto the street that led to the coffee shop. A car that had been lagging behind her for the last three or four minutes turned as well. She narrowed her eyes.

Through her rearview mirror, a dark sedan appeared—not unlike the one she had watched from her kitchen window. *Surely not!* Her imagination was working overtime. She straightened in the seat and pressed the accelerator. Cabot Falls must be filled with dark sedans steering a clear path to town. Why did her mind immediately spring to something sinister?

The coffee shop lay just ahead. She turned into the pickup lane and felt a surge of relief to recognize a Cabot Falls police car. It was the only one in the queue, and inside was Ryan Quimby, who had a regular hankering for the shop's cream doughnuts. There was no mistaking his ginger hair and square shoulders.

It looked like the sedan would turn in as well but then quickly angled back toward the street. Had he planned to follow her but spotted the police car and changed course? Or had she only imagined it? Whoever it was continued leisurely down the street. She strained to see a license plate. No numbers, but clearly it wasn't a Vermont plate.

She pulled up close to the young officer's patrol car and tapped her horn. Recognizing her behind him, he grinned broadly and put up a hand in greeting. She rolled down the window and gestured for him to do the same. "Can we meet inside?" she yelled as rain slanted in. She followed him as he bypassed the drive-through window and pulled around in front.

"Sorry to bother you," she said once they were both inside.

"I was hoping to get my coffee in the dry comfort of my vehicle," he said, eyeing her quizzically. "But, for you, I'm willing to brave the elements."

"Espresso Macchiato," she told the barista. "And a Cinnamon Dolce Light to go." She smiled at Ryan. "I'm picking up something for Marla, but when I saw you, I thought we should talk."

They found a booth and set down their purchases. Officer Quimby went in search of extra napkins. "I suppose you're wanting to know what we have learned in our investigation," he began when he was settled.

"Well, yes." She frowned and took a sip of her drink. *How lame will it sound to say I think someone was watching the house? That someone might have followed me to town? Someone with an out-of-state license plate.* That part didn't make any sense at all, even if the rest of it did. She unfolded a napkin and took another slow drink.

"We haven't been able to identify the partial fingerprint we lifted from your patio door yet," Officer Quimby said.

"Uh-huh," she replied somewhat dispiritedly. Their intruder was likely someone with more curiosity than experience. She fell silent.

"I understand you paid José Martinez a visit," Officer Quimby said. "He came to see me and explained the situation. You must have been very convincing." He gave her an appraising glance and rubbed his jaw, a sign that something bothered him. "Anything happening at your end?"

She hesitated. What good would it do to send him chasing after a dark sedan with out-of-state plates, someone who may or may not have been watching her house? Who may or may not have been following her? She felt suddenly foolish and sighed. "Still grasping at straws, coming up dry," she replied. "I better get to the library. Jim is taking the kids to a basketball game tonight, and dinner has to be ready early."

Officer Quimby nodded thoughtfully, as though something

particular were on his mind. He slid out of the booth. "Well, we'll just keep digging," he said. "We'll get to the bottom of it."

There was no sign of the dark sedan when she left for the library, but the rain had settled into a steady drizzle. When she arrived, she took a seat near Marla's desk and waited for the librarian to finish helping a customer in the reference section.

"Oh, you're a lifesaver," Marla said with hushed enthusiasm as she reached for the paper cup. "Is it still raining? You look a bit bedraggled."

Sofia put a hand to her damp hair and groaned.

"Never mind. You look fine," Marla said, grinning. "Come on." She wagged her head to a small round table that held several volumes and a raft of papers.

"I can't stay long," Sofia said. "I have a huge order of macaroons to bake, and I have to go shopping first. As the poet laments, I have 'miles to go before I sleep.' I was hoping you might turn up something about Ernest Haynes."

"I checked," she began. "I found Ernest's four brothers, all apparently well connected in business, and learned that his mother was the daughter of a coal magnate. His father was a wealthy banker originally from San Francisco. But all my attempts to follow the previous generations have resulted in dead ends."

"He's sure proud of his aristocratic background, whatever it is," Sofia said with a sigh. "But you said you'd found something about that Hunter character Adelia Long wrote about. What's got your antennae raised?"

Marla's perceptive brown eyes narrowed.

"Something I found in the 'Brevities' section of the *Daily Alta California* for May 1882. It's a wonder that I happened on it. There's a ton of nineteenth-century newspapers from that part of the country." She read from the printout: "'J. Wellington Hunter, owner of the Golden Cone, was hanged for the murder of Guadalupe Hernandez of Sonora. He was the son of William Lytton Hunter, one-time Sacramento hotel magnate who was convicted of fraud in 1869.'"

Sofia's pulse quickened. Adelia's account was set in that part of the country.

"I began tracing this William Hunter," Marla said. "He made a fortune operating gambling houses and brothels in Sacramento and later San Francisco. Seems he was infamous for his cutthroat tactics and was knifed while serving a lengthy prison sentence." She sighed. "Like father, like son."

Gambling houses in Sacramento. Hadn't Adelia Long written that Wylie Hunter was suspected of such activity even while working a claim on Mok Hill? Wylie could be a nickname. Could William Lytton Hunter and Wylie Hunter be one and the same? Sofia grasped Marla's arm. "What about this J. Wellington Hunter, William's son? Any children you've been able to trace?"

"A later article in the *Daily Alta* says he had two sons who went East around the turn of the century." Marla raised an eyebrow. "No doubt they would want to get as far away from the scandals of their father and grandfather as possible. But look, Sofia." She tapped her finger on the computer screen. "Their names were Anders and Ernest, and their surnames were officially changed from Hunter to Haynes."

"You don't suppose . . ." Sofia breathed.

Marla shrugged. "It's a long shot. But whether there's any connection to Ernest Haynes or not, I'll bet you anything that William Lytton Hunter and Wylie Hunter could be the same man."

It was too bizarre to be true. Wasn't it? Sofia's mind whirled. Was the Ernest she knew a decendent of the Ernest Haynes who fled California to avoid a scandal that went all the way back to the Gold Rush of 1849? She searched her mind to remember. It was Matthew who had blurted out in Ernest's hearing that the bag of gold came from "Muck Hill" and that it was all there in the diary! *Muck Hill . . . Mok Hill.* And Ernest had stopped cold like a deer in the headlights.

"You are amazing, Marla Dixon," Sofia said. "But I have to get home." Hurrying away, she called over her shoulder, "I owe you a year's worth of Cinnamon Dolce Lights."

14

Mokelumne Hill California
October 1849

$\mathcal{T}$he news of the robbery heralded so conspicuously by Calvin Means spread rapidly through the camp. Matters turned darker as more reports of theft surfaced. Miners began hiding their gold, looking on one another with suspicion, and keeping their pistols oiled and ready.

"The spirit of excitement and goodwill that marked our first days at Mok Hill is gone," Adelia said, more to herself than to Hoke, who had joined the line of men waiting outside her cook tent.

"It don't make sense," Hoke said, scratching his head and consuming his plate of biscuits and ham. "Everybody's making a tolerable day's wage, and there's still plenty of gold waiting to be plucked up."

A good amount of gold dust was also dropping into the thick glass jug on the makeshift table beneath Adelia's simple sign: *Ham and biscuits $1.00, beans 50 cents, eggs with ham $2.00.* The miners seemed happy to dole out their pinches, one pinch of gold dust being equal to a dollar. She hoped she was asking a fair price. *I'll be better able to gauge costs when the supply wagon comes*, she thought. *It had better be soon. There's only a scoop or two of flour left for tomorrow's baking.*

She watched Hoke and the other men head for the diggings,

packs loaded and pistols stuck in their belts. She grieved for the unhappy state of affairs. These men were all her friends. She didn't want to think that one of them might be a thief.

Just as she began to put the foodstuffs away and close up her little kitchen, a small figure appeared at the edge of the tent. Isaac. She had told him to come by and get more biscuits for his mother, and here he was. She motioned to him to sit beside her, and tentatively he advanced, with head hung low. *Could Isaac be sneaking into the men's belongings and stealing their gold?* Her mind rejected the idea. The thefts had all the marks of grown-up greed. Isaac had swiped a couple of biscuits but only for the love of his mother.

"Good morning, Isaac," she called cheerily.

The boy raised his head slightly and cast her a fleeting glance before looking away. He sat down and held his battered hat on his small, knobby knees. He was a picture of utter dejection and penitence. Adelia's heart melted. She reached into the pocket of her apron and withdrew two biscuits she had saved for Charity. As she held them out to the boy, she asked, "How is your mother this morning, Isaac?"

Small lips trembling, he made no move to accept the biscuits. Thin, wispy hair strayed over his forehead as he fidgeted with hands that were red and chapped. "I . . . I'm sorry," he managed. "I took the biscuits yesterday. I know it was wrong. You don't have to give me any more." He started to get up, as though to leave.

"Wait," Adelia said. "I know you did it for your mother. How is she today?"

His eyes brightened. "She is better now," he said. Then, in a sudden burst of childish exuberance, he added, "Last night she made porridge for Pa and me."

"I'm so glad, Isaac. Please take these." She put the little wrapped package of biscuits in his hands, delighted about Charity's change of heart. Adelia gave the youngster a stern look. "You must promise never to take anything again without permission."

Isaac pressed his lips together. His wide, blue eyes were rimmed by remarkably long lashes that swept his thin cheek. "I promise, ma'am," he said. "I—I never took nothin' before, but Ma was so sad and sick, I thought . . ." One fat tear rolled down his cheek.

"I know you did it for her, but that is no excuse." She softened her tone a bit. "Do you understand?"

"Yes ma'am," he said contritely. He paused and looked up at her again. "How come?" he asked, his pale eyebrows knit together.

"How come what?"

"How come you didn't tell—my ma and pa, I mean."

Adelia was quiet for several seconds. "I knew why you took the biscuits, and I hoped you would admit it. Now, can I hold you to your promise?" She didn't have to say that should he get in trouble again, he would most certainly have to deal not only with her, but also his parents.

He bobbed his head up and down vigorously and wiped his cheek with his ragged sleeve.

"Go along now," she said gently. "Your pa will be needing you at the diggings." She'd seen his small form down at the river, washing gravel in a metal pan while his father clawed and poked the rocky shore. She watched him go, saddened to think that Isaac should be in school, learning his letters, and munching happily on a packed lunch and playing with his friends at recess. Such was the life she and Quinton had enjoyed growing up in Kanesville, but Isaac had been thrust into an adult world he couldn't hope to understand.

The camp was growing quiet, miners having headed to the river for the day's work, when Calvin Means strode up to her cook tent. He had an old-fashioned Colt revolver and a huge Bowie knife slung to his belt. In his thick fingers, he carried an empty tin plate, which he stretched toward her for filling. She wished she had closed up sooner. But here he stood, red beard bristling his jaw, bloodshot eyes intense.

"I'll take the ham and eggs," he said gruffly, reaching for his pouch.

Obviously he wasn't robbed of all his gold. She thought about his drunken sobs when he'd come raging out of his tent, claiming someone had stolen his gold and his daddy's watch. She'd seen that timepiece before on a silver chain attached to his trouser pocket. Now and then, Calvin liked to bring it out and read the time aloud just to show off the handsome piece. He might easily have dropped the watch while panning for gold. Or lost it in one of the games of chance that were becoming more and more popular among miners when boredom set in.

Adelia drew in her breath and reached for the heavy fry pan. "It's late, and I don't have much left," she said and ladled the last scoop of eggs onto his plate along with a slab of ham.

Means peered around her to the secluded place behind the tent where Siba and Quinton sat on a log bench. In his convalescence, Quinton had taken avidly to his sketchbook and was showing Siba his drawings as they ate from tin plates. Means stared at the two young men through narrowed eyes. "I seen that Indian skulking around! Everybody knows them savages will steal a man blind."

Adelia had worried for Siba since he'd come to work along-side Quinton and Hoke. She'd warned him to be careful and to stay out of sight as much as possible. Indians were the first to be suspected of wrongdoing, followed by foreigners and native Californians. Now, someone had been stealing from miners' tents, and Siba could be in danger. She straightened to her full five feet six inches and folded her arms across her apron. "Siba is not skulking. He's working for us. My brother would have lost his claim if it wasn't for Siba." Indignation burned in her. "Besides, everybody knows Indians don't care about gold dust. They ask only for the means to live now that their hunting grounds have been destroyed."

The prospector glared at her, his red face becoming even redder than the disheveled hair under his hat. He had always shown respect for her, as miners in general did where women were concerned. Most viewed them with a kind of reverence. They pined for their families and for the familiar contours of small-town life, and a woman in the camp inspired thoughts of home. Many thought of their journey west as an extended business trip, which would detain them no longer than the brief time necessary to gather a pile of gold and hurry back to their wives and children.

Would that respect be compromised now as men grew greedy and untrusting? Sputtering, Means dropped two pinches into Adelia's jar and stepped back only slightly, pursing cracked lips beneath his red mustache. "Wylie's gonna be watching for anyone with slippery fingers," he muttered. "Injuns 'specially." He cast another black glance at Siba.

Adelia watched Calvin head toward his pack mule, grumbling under his breath. Lawbreakers would not be tolerated. Wylie Hunter would be gathering his team of vigilantes to consider how to proceed. She felt a shiver, remembering reports of "instant justice" that had filtered among the miners along the northern river camps. In places like Middle Bar, French Hill, and Rattlesnake Gulch, justice took the form of floggings, fines, expulsions, and even lynching.

Adelia closed up the cook tent and headed for her wagon with pots and utensils to be washed. Seeing her, Quinton rose, swaying as he attempted to help her with the load. He had made good strides, but he was still weak and besieged by nighttime fevers. "It's okay," she called and was relieved when he dropped back down on the bench and picked up his sketch pad.

"I've been practicing on Siba," he said as she came alongside. He turned the pad toward her, a look of pride on his face. A swirl of curly hair falling over his forehead gave him a childish aspect that touched Adelia.

She put the utensils on the ground and took up the sketch. It was an excellent likeness of Siba, rail thin and sinewy with black air hanging loose from the raglike band that circled his strong forehead. Muscular brown arms were crossed over his bare chest as if in contemplation. Much as Quinton tried to get him to wear a shirt, Siba seemed determined to be free of it. She studied the Indian's serious eyes in their hollowed-out cavities, eyes that seemed to look beyond the horizon to something longed for or dreaded.

"It's very good, Quint," Adelia said, thrilled that her brother had not lost his artistic ability. She smiled at Siba, whose face remained impassive but for a quick dart of light in his eyes. He and Quinton had become fast friends, often talking late into the night before the campfire.

"The young one is gifted of the Great Spirit," Siba said, the spark brightening in his deep-set eyes. "But the Great Spirit gave him no skill with this." He lifted his tomahawk from a strap on his leg and gave Quinton an unrestrained grin. "Throws like woman," he added, then turned a sheepish face away.

Siba spoke excellent English, but Adelia was sure that he occasionally lapsed into speech without article or pronoun just for the fun of it. "He's captured your likeness exactly," she told him, laughing. The ancient superstition that a likeness stole the spirit had likely been driven from Siba's mind, raised as he was in white society. And he could put his foot in his mouth as well as anyone. But she forgave him his remark about women. She would miss him when it was time to leave Mok Hill.

Several sketches lay scattered on the ground near the wooden bench where Quinton and Siba had been sitting. One of them showed a raging Calvin Means, fists raised, red hair bristling beneath his hat. Adelia studied it with concern.

Following her gaze, Quinton asked, "What was Calvin all fired up about this time? Was he drunk again?"

Some of the miners had brought whiskey into the camp. For the most part, they imbibed temperately while there, but Means had been known to overindulge and cause a ruckus. "He claims someone broke into his tent and helped themselves to his gold," Adelia said. "It's more likely that he spent it all on liquor, but—" She stopped, remembering the man's rage about Indians. "He's looking for someone to blame." She caught Siba's eye and held it. "Best to keep out of his way."

"I am not afraid," Siba said gravely. After a few seconds, he rose from the bench. "I should get to work." Shoulders set, he quietly disappeared into the woods.

Adelia turned to Quinton. "He must be very careful," she said in a whisper. "He must stay behind the wagon and out of sight of the camp."

"I don't know what we'd have done without him," Quinton said, picking up the sketch of Siba once more and holding it out proudly. "I wish I could get back to the diggings, but I do have some good news, Sister." Color rose in Quinton's cheeks, his little boy optimism shining in upturned eyes.

Adelia felt herself smiling, cast back in time to their childhood and guess-what games. It was wonderful to see his face alight with hope. "I can't imagine," she said, laughing.

"I've been selling some of these rude sketches," he said. "Can you believe it? Jack Smithson gave me five pinches for a drawing of his mangy old mule. And Mr. Rutters paid almost as much for a portrait of himself to send back home. Oh, Addie, at least I'm doing something to earn my keep!"

"I always told you what a great artist you are. I'm not surprised that you've captured the interest of the miners." She dropped down beside him. "We're going to be all right. There are more ways to earn gold than panning in the river. You can sell your art, and feeding the miners is proving very fruitful for me. I can make sixteen dollars a week for every man I cook for." She paused. "Papa would be proud of us, don't you think?"

Adelia left Quinton to his drawings and finished setting her campsite to rights and tucking her pots and pans neatly beneath her wagon. Presently, she heard the sound of horses clomping up the slope, followed by a wave of welcoming voices. The supply wagon from Sacramento was rumored to have left the neighboring camp and was headed their way. Miners were eager to buy, not just food supplies, but pickaxes, pans, boots, and shirts. Excitedly, she headed toward the center of camp, brushing moist strands of hair from her cheeks. She tied a clean apron over her blue muslin dress with the sack of gold dust tucked safely inside.

The supply wagon was a long, burgeoning vehicle pulled by a team of horses and driven by a small, barrel-chested man in waistcoat and vest. Two heavily laden mules carrying sacks of flour and grain were tied onto the back of the wagon. Adelia joined the cluster of men, who politely made room for her. A few doffed their hats, issuing cheerful good mornings.

Adelia stepped back to watch the loud negotiations. Mild oaths and cries of "Highway robbery!" issued from the startled miners who were paying eighteen dollars for a cradle, five dollars for a pickax, two dollars for a shirt, and ten dollars for a pair of boots. Coffee was going for five dollars a pound, a jar of pickles for one dollar, and a pint of molasses for fifty cents.

The merchant, who looked every bit the part of a successful businessman in his dark suit and bowler hat, answered each complaint in a pleasant English accent, occasionally twisting a dark mustache and nodding his head.

"I've never seen such prices," Adelia said indignantly when it was her turn. "How can you charge so much for a pound of coffee? And ten dollars for a bag of cornmeal is outrageous!" Of course she knew she couldn't compare these costs to prices they paid in the East, but it seemed storekeepers and teamsters were the ones getting rich on the backs of miners. The thousands of rushers coming in all needed provisions and equipment as well as a few comforts, and they were rife with gold.

"We pay stiff prices too, madam," he responded good-naturedly. "Goods coming into the levee at Sac City get bid up the minute they arrive."

The merchant's little black eyes took on a twinkle as he jumped down from the wagon with the supplies she requested. Women were a rare sight, and he had spotted not only Adelia, but also Charity Reed heading toward the clearing. It was obvious the man was delighted to see something other than scraggly beards and dirty britches. It was odd how men's faces would light up at the sight of someone moving gracefully in a colorful dress that rippled on the wind.

"I daresay getting these supplies delivered way out here in the wilderness does cost a pretty shilling," he said amiably. "But I'll be glad to carry your complaints to the merchant in charge, my lady."

"More swindler than merchant!" she charged hotly. "You can tell him Miss Adelia Long is far from pleased and that the quality of these supplies had better be very good indeed."

"Now, madam. Surely you can understand that Mr. Harte has to make a living too. He's bound to pay a high price for the wares brought in."

Adelia stared, transfixed. Had he said Harte? Did she hear correctly? It was a common enough name that might be spelled in several different ways—Hardt, Heart, Hart, or . . . Harte! There could be any number of men with that particular surname. Couldn't there?

"Will you require any utensils, my lady?" the merchant asked as he placed her bags and crates on the ground. He reached into the wagon and drew out a number of ladles, spoons, and knives.

She stared at the round little man with the swirling mustache as though the answer to her questions could be defined in his features. After a few seconds of stunned silence, she stammered a reply. "And who might this lucky merchant without a heart be?"

"Ah, he's a proper gentleman, he is," he responded. "A fine figure of a man for a Yank, and I never knew him to charge more than his due."

"Would he perhaps go by the name of Augustus Harte?" she asked just above a whisper.

"This enterprise belongs to one A. Langley Harte. Can't tell you more than that. I'm just a driver hired to carry supplies to the miners and to splendid ladies such as yourself." He gave a little bow and doffed his bowler hat. "If there's nothing else I can get for you, I'll bid you a good day." He turned neatly on small feet and hefted a rucksack from his wagon with an ease that belied his bulk.

When the last customer had been served, she stood in the swirling dust and watched the wagon disappear from view. Even when Charity came alongside and tucked a hand inside her elbow, she remained rooted to the spot.

Was it possible that the man she had loved and lost was only a few miles away, operating a business in the great untamed West? The words he had uttered with such fierce hope echoed in her mind: *Someday I will build something of value. I will do something worthy of life and living.*

How worthy was relieving helpless miners of their hard-won gold dust? And had he been so busy building his fortune that he couldn't forward a letter to her in all these long months? Irrational anger built inside her and with it a hollow longing that she couldn't name.

15

Mokelumne Hill, California
October 1849

$\mathcal{Q}$uinton's health continued to improve until he could spend a few hours each day working the claim that still yielded as much as fifteen dollars on a good day. There were those lean days, of course, when a meager two or three dollars might be coaxed from the river. When he wasn't at the diggings, he was busy working with Hoke to build a cabin in preparation for the coming cold and finding ready buyers for his sketches. Indeed, his art was becoming more profitable than panning or working the cradle.

Adelia's days also were filled with labor, consuming her time and energies. She would wake before dawn to stoke the fire, set the dough to rising, and prepare pan after pan of scrambled eggs and potatoes. More and more gold seekers had joined Mok Hill, filling it with tents and lean-to shacks, and Adelia's cook tent drew more and more hungry miners.

The men who subsisted on hastily consumed beans and coffee were terribly undernourished. She had treated many who suffered from scurvy. It made Adelia feel good to be able to offer real cooked meals made from bacon, salt pork, rice, and even vegetables.

The daily drudgery left little time for dreaming of the future or pining over the past. Yet in the days since the supply wagon had come through, Adelia couldn't help but puzzle over what she had heard from the driver about one A. Langley Harte—proprietor, proper gentleman. "A fine figure of a man for a Yank."

"Langley" might be a middle name or a vintage family moniker unknown to me, she thought. *More likely, the Harte operating a thriving business in Sac City is someone I've never met, a clever entrepreneur who cares little for the pressing needs of the miners.*

But what if *her* Augustus was the owner of the enterprise? If he had ever been hers, he had forgotten her altogether. *Foolish girl!* she chided herself. *Can you not let it go?*

"A penny for your thoughts," Charity said, leaning against a tree from whose branches pots and utensils hung in readiness. She had become Adelia's right hand in the cook tent and also had taken to washing and mending the miners' clothes. When he wasn't at the diggings with his father, Isaac helped tote water barrels to and from the river.

"I daresay my thoughts may not be worth as much," Adelia said, glad for Charity's company. The woman who had once been unable to rise from her bed now set her delicate frame to her tasks without complaint. Older by a dozen years, the dark-haired, almond-eyed woman brightened Adelia's days. She had grown less gaunt, thanks to the tasty pies the two concocted together. The miners who remembered those baked by wives and sweethearts especially desired homemade pies. Adelia and Charity could sell as many pies at three dollars each as they could turn out.

Adelia leaned back next to Charity, sighing. The sky was a blue canopy—wide, endless, with a few wispy clouds drifting by. She imagined they were the same puffs of water vapor that would fling themselves all the way across the plains to Iowa. "Do you ever wonder what might have been if we hadn't left home?" she asked. "Or what we might be doing at this very minute?"

Charity wrapped her arms across her stomach and matched Adelia's sigh. "I suppose I'd be working my fingers to the bone trying to grow enough vegetables to get us through the long Minnesota winters. And Hannibal would keep plowing those stubborn fields." She paused and gave Adelia a sidelong look. "Or I might be turning into a sodden lump, the way I was on the overland journey, and might be still if it wasn't for you. I'm grateful God sent you to me."

Adelia lowered her head, humbled by Charity's praise. She had wanted only to be useful, to make a difference. Perhaps she had. At the same time, the mention of Minnesota caught her up sharply. She brushed away thoughts of Augustus. "You would have come around," she said warmly, remembering how devastated Charity had been by little Hannah's death, how she nearly lost sight of Isaac. "My papa always said it's a terrible thing to lose a child."

"To lose anyone you love," Charity added. "I'm sorry about your parents, Addie." In the quietness that followed, a few busy sparrows ruffled the leaves above their heads. "I almost forgot how lucky I am to have Isaac—and Hannibal. My husband can be too serious at times, but he's a good man." She was quiet for a moment and then turned thoughtful eyes on her friend. "Is there anyone back home waiting for you, Addie?"

Adelia felt something sharp pierce her heart. "Oh no. That is, not anymore." She took a breath and let it out in an ironic little sigh. "There was this man from Minnesota. We met one spring when his regiment passed through Kanesville." She fell silent as a vision of Augustus, tall and resplendent in his uniform, filled her mind's eye. She could almost hear the strains of the waltz that was playing that night and feel the warmth of his arm circling her waist as they glided over the polished floor.

Had it really been almost two years? He had driven her home

in a borrowed carriage, lamenting the fact that he had none of his own. The night had been balmy with a crescent moon barely the size of a fingernail. Innumerable stars had blurred the heavens with their abundance. Augustus had spread a blanket over her billowing lavender skirt with such tenderness that she had felt breathless.

In her gloved hand, she'd held a single white daisy that he had stopped to pick along the way. "You are worth the finest flowers, tinged with the dew of heaven," he had said gallantly as he presented the flower to her.

From anyone else, such syrupy words would sound contrived, but Augustus was an unusual man. *What woman could resist a man who spoke like a poet?* she thought. *But then again, were there others who elicited such musical tributes from his lips?*

"I wish this daisy could be a bouquet of roses," he had added. "One day, I'll make that wish come true, and I hope you'll be there to receive it."

"It's a long way from Minnesota to Mok Hill," Charity said gently, interrupting Adelia's thoughts. "Maybe you'll have a letter when the express comes through." When Isaac appeared on the horizon with two buckets on a long pole, she gathered her basket of clean laundry. "I best be getting back," she said. "Hannibal will want his dinner." She paused. "Besides, it looks like Eagle Eye might be wanting a word with you. Hannibal does not trust that one!"

It occurred to Adelia that Charity's name for the self-styled leader of the camp was similar to Siba's name for him—Hawk Eyes. She turned to see Wylie Hunter mounted on his tall black stallion poised at the edge of the wood. She wasn't surprised to see him. He often rode up at odd times during the day or night, sharp eyes watchful and looking less like a miner than a dude, as the men referred to greenhorns and merchants who visited the camps.

It was rumored that Wylie had purchased a hotel in Sacramento that was turning rich profits. It wasn't unusual for miners to turn to other, less laborious endeavors in pursuit of gold. But Adelia had a bad feeling where Wylie was concerned. He came and went, often when the miners were gone to the diggings. He felt it was his due to inspect every tent or shack on Mok Hill. His own claim was being operated by paid workers. It must be unusually rich for Wylie to have accrued a fortune so quickly.

He continued to linger at the edge of the clearing, his horse stamping impatiently in the partial shade and nibbling clumps of grass. She drew in her breath and wondered what he wanted, for he was staring directly at her. He was watching the camp and her in particular as though something were on that sharp and cunning mind of his.

She had washed her hair that morning, basking in the small privacy the creek afforded and enjoying the sunshine on her aching shoulders. She had put on a clean apron over her plaid calico and was, she supposed, at least presentable. She wondered why that mattered and why, at the same time, a sense of dread crept over her.

When Charity and Isaac disappeared around a bend, Hunter began a slow trot toward her. He dismounted and approached, a solemn expression on his face. "Sorry to bother you, but this is a matter of utmost importance." He drew his arms across his chest and regarded her through narrowed eyes. "You are aware that there have been reports of thievery in the camp?"

Adelia took a step back, unnerved. He was dressed more like a miner today but for the bowler hat that didn't quite match his shirt and duck trousers. A pistol was stuck prominently from the holster slung below his narrow waist. Rumor had it that he had used it more than once to settle disputes at the place he now managed in Sac City.

She squared her shoulders. "I'm aware of the thefts."

"And are you aware that the Indian who works for you was seen skulking around the camp the day Calvin Means was robbed?"

She bit her tongue to tamp down her anger. "I was there as well, and I assure you that Siba was not skulking. He was engaged in conversation with my brother." Before he could interrupt, she continued. "You have no right to accuse Siba other than your own prejudice." She heard herself fairly spit the words.

"You're a fool to trust him—to trust any Indian! You don't know them. Savages, all of them."

"Have you not heard how the Cahuilla supported a U.S. Army expedition and defended them against attacks by the Utes—their common enemy? And how they joined us in fighting off the Luiseños at the Temecula Massacre?" Adelia crossed her arms over her chest. "Siba is a Cahuilla. They are not savages. Indians are not all savages—Siba least of all."

Wylie tightened his jaw, as though cutting off a quick retort. In seconds, his features turned placid, and he appeared almost to smile. "Well, whoever is guilty of these thefts will be judged swiftly and decisively, I assure you. But I came to see you this morning on quite a different errand. The men say there's something special about your cooking." He tempered his usual frown. "I thought I'd better see if they know what they're talking about."

Adelia placed both hands on her hips and drew in a settling breath. There was a charisma about Wylie Hunter that made him a formidable foe. He was a man who knew his power and used it to his advantage. "Breakfast is long since over, sir," she stated firmly. "But I can heat up some eggs and ham, and there might be a biscuit or two left over. That is, if you can pay the price of three dollars."

"Three dollars!" he mimicked, drawing a hand across his square jaw. "I think the lady is becoming something of a mercenary." His tone was gruff and accusatory, but a glint entered his eye, and a smirk tugged at his mouth.

"Not at all, I assure you," she responded. "With eggs at one dollar each, flour at four dollars, and coffee even higher, three dollars is a fair price to exact for a hearty meal."

Wylie stroked his chin once more and gave a small mock bow. "So it must be," he said. He rested an arm on a tent pole and watched her closely as she prepared his requested meal. "I admire your cunning, madam," he said. "After all, the men need to eat, and there's plenty of gold for the price."

"I do not wish to be cunning," she said, turning scrambled eggs onto the one clean dish that remained from breakfast. "I wish only to provide for myself and my brother, who has been quite ill. However, he, too, is making good use of his recuperation by plying his skill with the sketchbook. Like everyone else, we work to support ourselves."

He smiled and pressed a little closer to her work area. "No offense," he said quickly. "On the contrary, I was thinking that you have the makings of a real entrepreneur." He cocked his head, sharp interest in his features. "A woman after my own heart," he added.

Adelia averted her eyes and scraped the last of the ham from the skillet. He was standing far too close—close enough that she could smell something cloyingly sweet. Hair oil perhaps. She stepped back and, in the attempt, tripped on a large bag of potatoes. She pitched forward and would have fallen had Wylie not quickly caught her. She could hear him breathe. An unnamed fear washed over her.

A sudden pounding of hooves signaled someone's approach. She pulled away from Wylie's grasp, heart thumping as the lone rider approached.

He sat very tall in the saddle and wore a wide hat that shrouded his face as he leaned forward. He was headed straight for Adelia's cook tent and came forward at a slow trot. Adelia turned her attention gratefully to the stranger who had unwittingly stopped whatever might have happened. He must want to purchase breakfast, for he had removed his hat and was striding toward them in a pair of leather breeches, a light shirt, and a string tie beneath a dark coat. She swept her hair back and was prepared to lift the iron skillet to the fire when something in the rider's face stopped her. Something about those clear golden eyes and the straight blond hair falling over his forehead.

Long legs striding, arms hanging at his sides, he fixed his eyes first on her, then on Wylie, who stood staring. There was no mistaking Augustus Harte. He was thinner, his hair bleached by sun or age, but the eyes that Adelia remembered with such longing shone in the smooth planes of his face.

He paused, reins in hand, and stared fixedly at Wylie. There was nothing of greeting in his aspect—only cool disdain as he faced the stranger, who must be no stranger at all.

Abruptly, and without a word spoken by either man, Wylie turned on his heel, mounted his horse, and headed for the woods behind her cook tent, the horse's hooves crunching on the gravelly ground.

16

Cabot Falls, Vermont
Present Day

By the time Sofia arrived with her groceries, Vanessa was home and munching on a bag of organic baby carrots. Definitely not the snack of choice for Matthew or Luke, who were heading home from the bus stop. "Hi, sweetheart. Have a good day?" Sofia dropped three bulging paper sacks on the kitchen table and gave her daughter a hug.

"It was okay, except for chemistry." Vanessa wrinkled her nose. "I can't understand what Auntie Rosa and Auntie Gina find so fascinating about stuff like that." She shrugged. "What's in the slow cooker?"

"Your dinner. Pork roast with vegetables. Good thing I got to the carrots before you did."

"I want to fit into my new blue dress by next week," she said by way of explanation and began helping Sofia put the groceries away.

Matthew pushed open the door and slammed it behind him. Dampness had coiled his dark hair into ringlets, and his shoelaces hung loose like spaghetti gone awry. He tossed his backpack onto the table and flung his jacket off. "Mom, where's my jersey?"

"It's in the dryer. And take that stuff to your room. We need the table for dinner." Nothing excited Matthew more than basketball. What he lacked in height he made up for in pure spunk and tenacity. "You'll have time to change for the game after dinner," she yelled after him. When he reappeared in the kitchen in record time, wearing his jersey, she wasn't at all surprised.

The late afternoon sped by with pleasant chaos as the children arrived home from school. Jim came home just before five and hurried to change his clothes. Vanessa helped Sofia set the table and arrange vegetables on the platter. Everyone vied for dinner and conversation, and soon the meal ended. The noisy hubbub continued until it was time for them to head off for the basketball game.

Jim looked tired. The dark shadows beneath his eyes hadn't disappeared completely since his illness. Sofia wished they had some time to talk about their day, though she had determined not to mention the dark sedan. It would only worry him, and besides, it was likely a figment of her imagination that had nothing to do with her.

"We'll be home early," Jim said, zipping up the leather jacket that still made him look like a college athlete. He glanced at Matthew, who was hurrying everyone out the door. "Unless the Tigers and the Wolverines go into overtime." He kissed Sofia, fixing her intently with his blue gaze. "You'll call if you need me, right?"

"Promise," she said, giving him a mock salute.

"By the way, I asked Ryan Quimby to cruise by a few times tonight." He hurried out before she had time to protest.

She watched Jim drive off and felt a singular gratitude for her crazy, wonderful family. She finished clearing the table in preparation for baking. Wynter, whose duty it was to clear the dishes, had been given temporary reprieve. Sofia smiled, remembering the look of relief that flooded Wynter's rolling blue eyes and the happy toss of her long black hair as she bounded out to the car.

When all was quiet, she locked the back door and switched on the kettle. She set out butter and eggs to warm to room temperature and consulted her coconut macaroon recipe for the rest of the ingredients. That would include semisweet chocolate to melt in a double boiler. Heather said the chocolate-dipped variety were a favorite of her customers.

When the teapot's whistle blared, she poured herself a cup of tea and sat down to relax and think while the oven preheated. A lot had happened since discovering the strange bag of gold. Visa arrangements were working out for José Martinez. Marjorie Bennett would be coming for her Saturday art lesson. She had phoned early that morning to remind Sofia of her promise. "It's all right, isn't it? I can still come after—"

Sofia smiled, remembering how Marjorie had wept her penitence for gossiping to the newspaper. Sofia assured her she would be welcome.

"You've always been good to me," Marjorie had repeated before ringing off.

Now Sofia's cell phone beeped. "I'm passing your house. Everything all right there?" Officer Quimby's voice, always measured and reassuring.

She went to the window and waved, phone in hand. "Thanks for coming by," she said brightly. "All quiet here. I'm up to my ears in macaroons though."

"Excellent. I'll be making my Saturday rounds to Heather's bakery tomorrow, and I'll be sure to ask for one of your specialties." He waved and drove on.

Tomorrow is Saturday already? Sofia sighed. *A whole week since the gold was found—and lost.* Except for the early rush of curious neighbors after the news item came out, things had settled down, though an occasional call came in, like the one from Ella Fitzsimmons, president of Cabot Falls's most elite women's club.

"You must come and speak to our group, Mrs. Parker. Everyone is enthused to hear how you found such an exciting piece of history."

She had declined an early invitation but told Mrs. Fitzsimmons she might call her at a later time. With any luck, the fervor would die down. Like Adelia Long, Sofia marveled at the power of anticipated wealth to capture the mind and heart.

Those I have called friends grow more and more reclusive, Adelia had written, *hiding their valuables and keeping a ready grasp on their guns. There are no more cheery campfires, no singing. Obsessed with gold and the worry to keep it, they are changing before my eyes.*

Sofia drank the last of her tea and began mixing the ingredients for the macaroons. She could hear the rain pinging steadily against the drainpipe. Glad for the comforting heat of the oven, she wondered how Adelia had managed to cook over an open fire and bake pies under the trees.

In spite of illness and loss, the indomitable pioneer woman had used her skills to survive. She had done "something worthy," to use words from the journal. On top of that, she had found the time and heart to reach out to people in the camp who needed her. Sofia whipped the egg whites with renewed fervor. *One could learn a lot from history and its stalwart men and women,* she thought.

Just as she was about to pop the first cookie sheet into the oven, the front doorbell rang several times in succession. "Now what?" she said aloud as she removed her oven mitts. The ringing continued, insistent, punctuated, strong. Perplexed, she went into the living room.

Whoever it was certainly couldn't be planning to break in and burgle her house. Intruders weren't known to ring the bell. Irritated but curious, she drew aside the narrow curtain to see a man in an overcoat and a tweed Gatsby hat, head bent against the rain.

The caller hit the bell once more. Stepping back, he raised his head, revealing a pointed gray beard. Ernest Haynes. Why on earth had he chosen to come for his supplies at this hour, and without calling first? She opened the door, prepared to launch her stern objection.

"I have come for my property," a red-faced Ernest said without preamble. He set his jaw. His narrowed eyes were mildly bloodshot, and his usually florid face more flushed than she'd ever seen it. Flushed with anger? Or something else? "My paints," he continued, "and my porfl . . . portfolio." The man who boasted perfect grammar and diction was having trouble with the word. Had he been drinking?

Unnerved, Sofia said, "If you'll just wait there, I'll get your things." She wasn't about to invite him in, not in that condition. She began to close the door—firmly and definitely—when Ernest lurched forward, pushing the door with both hands. He leered at her with angry gray eyes.

"Stop!" Sofia shouted. "What are you doing?" She felt herself thrust back. She tried to catch herself on the arm of the sofa, but instead she tripped and tumbled backward and down onto the cushion.

Haynes slammed the door behind him, looming over her and making it impossible for her to get up. She stared at the angry face with its comical goatee, the stray silver hairs poking out around his ears. She'd seen his indignation when his art wasn't appreciated to his satisfaction, or when someone he deemed inferior—like Marjorie Bennett—criticized him. But she hadn't seen this side of him, this physically domineering, ranting, half-drunk bully.

"I want that diary." He spoke in a low voice cut through with steel. "You're not going to ruin everything! Everything my family has built—ever'thing I'm building in this town!" He slurred this last rant and shook a finger in her face.

The diary! Marla had discovered a possible connection between the California Gold Rush and Ernest. She had hardly believed it could be true, but here he was, demanding the diary he had seen a week earlier as he stood in her kitchen. Pulse pounding, she prayed for calm.

"Mr. Haynes," she began. "You said you've come for your property. The diary to which you refer, however, is my property." *If only I could reach my cell phone*, she thought. But it was in the kitchen, along with the diary, which was still tucked inside the bread box.

Ernest seemed stunned, whether by her failure to obey instantly or by the calm she had achieved. He glowered down at her. He wasn't a big man, but he seemed enormous hovering over her. He swallowed, and a muscle in his temple throbbed visibly. "You have no right to ruin the reputation of my fam'ly," he slurred with something of a petulant child's rebuke. "That belongs to me! My family has protected it for more than a hundred years. I won't let you spoil it now."

She stared. So it was true. The bloodline of the infamous Hunters ran through the veins of the upstanding Boston Hayneses—all the way down to Ernest Wellington Haynes Jr., lately moved to Cabot Falls, Vermont. She drew in her breath. "Mr. Haynes," she began patiently, "didn't *you* take something that belongs to *me*? Wasn't it you who took the pouch?"

He frowned as though working out a puzzle in his not-quite-sober consciousness. "But those initials were his," he said, pushing out his jaw. "*W. H.* After all these years, I couldn't allow that despicb'le man to ruin our fam'ly name."

Not *V. N.* as she had thought, but *W. H.*, Wylie Hunter, who after being exiled from the goldfields had made a fortune operating gambling houses and brothels. According to the records, he had been ruthless in his tactics. And he had raised a progeny of equally grasping and immoral sons until a descendent had denounced the sordid life of his forebears. How sad that Ernest couldn't applaud his ancestor's courage instead of trying to hide any connection to the evils of previous generations. No one would have known about it if he hadn't made an issue of it. *Sad, foolish man! How did he hope to make things better this way?*

"Enough talk. I demand that you give it to me now!" He grabbed her by the arm, yanking her up to a standing position.

"Please, Mr. Haynes. You're hurting me. You're not thinking clearly. You don't want to do this."

But he had her firmly in his grasp, pinning her arm behind her back. Would he really hurt her? He hadn't produced a gun or a knife, but he was a great deal stronger than Sofia. *What can I do?*

And suddenly, a key turned in the front door lock, and Jim stood like an avenging angel in a leather jacket, blond curls dripping wet. "Let her go! Now!" The voice was a sonic boom.

Ernest cowered, stumbled, and fell onto the sofa into which he had earlier pushed Sofia. His face turned ghostly white, and the goatee trembled. He appeared to collapse, dropped his head, and pressed his hands to his temples.

Jim pulled Sofia into his arms. "Are you all right? Did he hurt you?"

"I'm all right. I'm not hurt." Relief washed through her as Jim held her securely. "He was after the diary," she whispered. "What Marla suspected is true."

When Officer Quimby stepped through the open door, Sofia and Jim were still staring down at a humiliated Ernest, who was likely more sober than when he pushed his way in.

Officer Quimby assessed the situation with professional calm. "Well, Mr. Haynes, it was you, wasn't it? You're the one who took the pouch. You also arranged for that two-bit crook to break in here. We got an ID on his fingerprint a little while ago, and when we caught him, he spoke up, loud and clear." Officer Quimby shook his head. "Tacky, Mr. Haynes, very tacky." He paused. "So where is it, then?"

Slowly, Ernest reached into the pocket of his overcoat and drew out the shabby leather pouch, the tag still attached to its drawstring. "I never wanted it. I just wanted . . ." He broke off helplessly as tears flowed from the eyes of the once-proud Ernest Wellington Haynes, aka Hunter.

17

Mokelumne Hill, California
October 1849

*C*ould it possibly be? Adelia braced herself against the tent pole and blinked several times to be sure she wasn't dreaming. *Augustus—my Gus!* He now stood before her, hat in hand, head bowed.

Her heart beat at the pace of a jackhammer, and her mouth went dry. So Gus had come west—likely months before she and Quinton had left Iowa. Why hadn't he let her know where he was? Yes, it took months for a letter to travel from California to the midsection of the country, but surely in all this time, he might have found some way to contact her if he cared at all. Yet here he stood, sun-browned, wearing a dapper suit and shiny boots, looking like the wealthy merchant he no doubt was.

When he looked up, she saw in those eyes a mixture of wonder and what might be shame. "Adelia? Is it really you, Adelia?" His voice was husky, and color rose in his cheeks.

She took a steadying breath and pretended nonchalance. "It is indeed," she heard herself say in a small voice. "I—I didn't know you were here—Augustus." She caught her trembling lip in her teeth.

"When my driver told me about you, I had to come," he said huskily. "How have you fared?" Polite, even-voiced, unsmiling. Maddening.

Adelia hid her work-roughened hands from his probing eyes and gave a brief recital of their decision to come west. "There were financial reverses after Papa died," she said. "Quint was eager to try his hand at panning for gold, and it was my decision to accompany him." Pride welled up, a pride that would not reveal that she had missed the man standing before her or was sorry he had abandoned her. She prattled on, inflating the account of finding gold at the diggings and of the money she had amassed cooking for the miners. "Hoke and Quint will build us a cabin before winter—"

She broke off, the hurt building up inside her. The truth was that the backbreaking work and the greed that had taken over many men's lives was wearing her down. She had begun to long for home, even to hold out hope that someday Gus would come for her. "So you need have no concern for us," she added, drawing her arms across her chest in stubborn resolve.

"Addie . . ."

He gave his head a slow shake. "Adelia," he corrected, as though he had overstepped some rule of decorum. Back East it would be "Miss Long" and "Mr. Harte," to be sure. But everything seemed to have changed in the wild reaches of California where there was little time to stand on ceremony. Gus appeared confused or frustrated.

"Please," he said, imploringly, "I need to explain." He shifted his weight and tied his chestnut roan to a nearby tree. "Could we not take a walk, away from everything, just for a few moments?"

"I—I have a lot of work to do." Adelia looked down, not wanting to see the hurt in his eyes. "It won't be long before the miners will be lining up for lunch, and I'll have to be ready."

"Please," he reiterated simply. He patted the bent neck of his horse and began walking along the road that led to the meadow. Turning, he cocked his head in an appealing gesture, and she joined him on the path, careful to keep a good distance between them. The midmorning sun streamed across the Sierras, and clouds drifted low and scant over the mountains. Tall grasses yellowed with the advance of early autumn, and ducks and geese flew noisily from stand to stand of timothy and chickweed.

Neither spoke for what seemed an eternity. Adelia heard the swish of her dress brushing against the weeds and their slow, deliberate footfalls on the path. Were they really walking side by side again, just as though the months had not intervened? As though nothing had happened?

"When the war was over, I had to make a decision," he began slowly, keeping his head bent. "I had nothing. Nothing at all. The farm was gone, my parents dead. I was alone in the world with nothing to offer anyone. Nothing to offer a woman. Nothing to offer . . . you." He fell silent for a moment. "I had to make something of myself. I had to try something—anything."

She said nothing as they moved slowly along. She had known his fortunes were small and hers nonexistent. But what did those things really matter if two people cared for each other as they had? As she thought they had. She swallowed against the hurt and heard him continue.

"When the news of a gold strike came, I decided it was a chance to recover something of what I had lost. I trekked across prairie, desert, and mountain on the back of a mule and dug gold from gravel along the Calaveras. Bone-weary labor, blistering sun, clouds of mosquitoes, and chilly dawns. After nearly a year, I had little to show for all that toil." He shook his head as though the memory pained him. "I tried to write several times, Addie. Truly, I did. But I was ashamed of myself, a broken prospector with gnarled hands and an empty purse. I couldn't tell you what I'd become."

She recalled the fierce longing in his voice when they had

ridden home in his carriage after the ball. *Someday I will build something of value. I will do something worthy of life and living.* She couldn't have guessed at the time what was in his mind or that he would travel nearly two thousand miles away from her in the process of finding that worthiness.

"But Providence smiled on me, Addie." He stopped on the path, took her hand, and looked directly into her eyes. "I sold my claim and bought half interest in a store to outfit the great stream of gold rushers. They needed everything, and I was able to supply them with tools and clothes and food. They had the money to pay." He paused, frowning, perhaps seeing something in her face that troubled him.

"So you have made your fortune," she said, surprised to hear the accusatory invective in her voice. "Flour and pork at one hundred and twenty-five dollars a barrel and molasses at ten dollars a gallon." It might be true that the price of goods arriving in the harbor at Sacramento was exorbitant, but something in her wanted to strike out at him. "You've gotten rich off the backs of the miners."

"We charge a fair price," he said gently, eyes dark with distress at her response. "We treat our customers well, for without them, we have no livelihood. As God is my witness, I have defrauded no man."

She knew she had cut him to the heart. Had he ever given her cause to think him anything but honest and hardworking? They were qualities that had drawn her to him in the beginning, along with his love of words and the poetry that sprang so easily to his lips. She pulled away, moving ahead on the path and setting her jaw. The silence hung heavy again, broken after a few paces by a covey of quail bursting from the high grass along the path. Unmindful of the woes and concerns that drove humans, the quail seemed to bring them both up short.

"Ah!" Gus said, watching the birds take flight. He turned to Adelia, his eyes full of wonder, the wonder that nature's beauty can evoke only in a receptive heart.

A smile came unbidden to Adelia's lips, and for a moment, she wished they could just forget the months of silence, the fear and concern, the sense of having been abandoned by love. It could be as though they had just met—here on this quiet path with nature's sweet innocence smiling on them.

Gus broke the silence, laying a gentle hand on her arm. "I miss home. I miss the quiet fields, the harvests that come not of man's striving but by God's gracious hand. I miss—" He stopped short. Perhaps he meant to say that he missed her most of all and simply couldn't. But his gaze was tender, his eyes full of concern. "Tell me, Addie, my dear Miss Adelia Long—who has never been but a short step away from my heart during all my travels—are you and Quinton all right? Do you need anything?"

Her arm tingled beneath his warm hand. She might easily have slipped into his embrace, overwhelmed to be so near him again after all this time, to know he was well and realizing the fulfillment of a dream. But she moved to dislodge his hand and drew a steadying breath, reconvening her pace. "Quint has been ill," she said matter-of-factly, "but he is better."

"Due to your excellent skill as a nurse, I am sure," Gus said admiringly. "No doubt many have been grateful for your knowledge of herbs and medicines and your generous heart."

She went on, eager to make him understand that she and her brother had done nicely without him. "Hoke and our friend Siba—he's a Cahuilla Indian who has befriended us—have done very well at the diggings. We have had some hardship, but like you, God has helped us."

"You are happy?" he asked softly. Not waiting for an answer, he asked, "Is there not something I can do for you? I worry about you.

This is a harsh country where gold makes enemies of good men."

"That is kind of you," she responded stiffly, "but we are fine, Quint and I. We have our friends, and we watch out for one another." She hadn't meant to deliberately exclude him as a friend.

He balled his fists at his sides in what might have been hurt or frustration. After a few awkward seconds, he asked, "And do you include Mr. Hunter among that number?"

"He was our guide on the trail and a worthy one, I must say," she responded quickly. "We might never have made it to California without his aid." She knew she sounded priggish, protecting a man she didn't really like or approve of. What was Gus's interest anyway? She thought back to the coolness with which he had regarded Wylie when he came upon them in the cook tent standing so close together. She recalled Wylie's narrowed eyes, the color flooding his cheeks at the sight of Gus. "And he helps keep order in the camp," she added, knowing she was adding fuel to the fire in Gus's mind.

"I must warn you to take the utmost care." He whipped the wide hat from his head and pierced her with stern eyes. "You should stay away from him. He is a danger to you and to everyone in the camp."

She brushed her hair back with a quick slice of her hand. "He has been nothing if not attentive to our needs." *Let Augustus be jealous. Let him see that another man could find me attractive.* She drew herself up sharply. "I do not understand your attitude. Indeed, I do not!"

"You don't understand," he began, then seeing the fire in her eyes, paused. "He has a certain reputation—"

"And since when have you been party to idle gossip? We are obliged to be grateful all the more to Mr. Hunter now that—" She paused. She hadn't meant to mention the thefts, the uncertainty, or her fear for Siba, but she rambled on. "There have been some thefts at Mok Hill, and a vigilance committee has been formed. Mr. Hunter, with his background as an officer in the army, is the most likely one to take the matter in hand. I must say that we are all quite grateful to him."

This last she said with a decided lift to her head, though she knew her statement was not exactly true. There were several who had begun to distrust Wylie, including herself. "And now, I really have to get back." She turned on her heel, forcing Gus to hasten to catch up.

They walked in silence, Gus deep in thought, brows drawn together. Had she hurt him sufficiently? Adelia knew she had reacted to his warning about Wylie from a position of wounded dignity and wondered about herself. *What is wrong with me? I've never been a vengeful person.* She might have asked exactly what he meant by "a certain reputation," but her pride had won out. She would not ask. She walked faster, and when they drew up alongside her wagon, she put out a stiff hand. "I'm very happy for your success, Augustus Harte, and I do thank you for coming."

"Adelia—" He stopped, apparently uncertain what to say, then repeated her name. "Addie—"

Before she looked away, she caught the anguish in his gaze. She steeled herself against any remorse. "It has been good to see you," she said with as much composure as she could muster, and she climbed into her wagon, drawing the flap closed behind her.

It seemed a long time before she heard him go, but eventually the beat of his horse's hooves grew fainter until she heard nothing at all. Nothing but the sad beating of her own heart. Why did he have to come just when she was learning to forget him? Well, he was headed back to his profitable business. He wouldn't seek her out again. Not after the way she had treated him.

Sleep came slowly that night. She was thankful for the first streaks of light and the task of cooking that would consume her time and engage her troubled mind for the next few hours. But first, she busied herself cleaning the wagon. She beat the old rag carpet fiercely and shook the quilts until her arms ached.

The previous day's conversation played over and over in her mind, refusing to be silenced. She imagined him, worn and tired, picking gold from clay and freezing river water and trudging back with his pack mule to a supper of cold coffee and beans. How gladly she would have written to encourage him if she had known. She would have described the Iowa fields fragrant beneath a cornflower sky. She would have told of news and events in Kanesville and said she was waiting for him.

But he had remained silent. Why should she believe he cared for her at all? If the wagon driver had not passed along her critique to his employer, would he ever have found her? Would he have looked for her if she hadn't rashly given her name? *You can tell him Miss Adelia Long is far from pleased and that the quality of these supplies had better be very good indeed.*

She grabbed a broom and began to sweep the wagon bed with ferocious strokes. So focused was she on dispatching the most minute particle and twig from around her wagon that she didn't hear Hoke ride up, didn't see him tether his old mule and stand watching her from a few yards away.

"Best be ordering yourself a new broom next time the supply wagon comes," he drawled good- naturedly. "You're beating the daylights out of that one."

"Oh, Hoke. I'm sorry. I didn't hear you."

He put a canteen to his mouth. "Gonna be powerful hot today."

She hadn't noticed but saw that his sunburned face was already sweaty, his gray hair stringy beneath his slouch hat. He'd likely been working on the cabin he and Quinton were building for her. His kindness touched her. She saw, too, that he was looking at her oddly, concern in his brown, red-rimmed eyes. She hesitated, wondering what was really on his mind.

"Everything all right here?" he asked, looking around. "Tuck Blane came by the diggings swearing that somebody made off with his crock of gold dust. Loaded for bear and blaming every man in sight. You seen anybody around Tuck's place?"

So Tuck Blane's tent had been robbed the morning before. It must have happened after he left for the diggings. She shrugged her shoulders. "Wasn't anyone around but Wylie. He came late for breakfast, then rode off."

Hoke narrowed his eyes and plucked idly at his mustache. "I don't trust that Wylie Hunter," he said. "He sure seems flush with gold, but the fellers working his claim told me that it's been dry for weeks. Yet Wylie's been throwing money around in that city hotel, trying to make a big name for himself."

Adelia supposed it was natural for miners, even Hoke, to be jealous of Wylie's success.

"Things is gettin' mighty trying," Hoke added, leaning against the trunk of a chestnut tree. "I don't like you being here alone. I told Quint to keep his eyeballs peeled. Siba and me can handle things at the claim."

"I'm not alone, Hoke. Charity and Isaac are here to help with the cooking. And Quint is around part of the time." Adelia sighed. Even Quinton seemed to be changing before her eyes from the sensitive youth who saw beauty in ordinary things to someone obsessed with gain and the worry to keep it.

"Siba better sleep out in the woods tonight," Hoke said, rubbing his stubbly jaw. "Hotheads would love to blame an Indian." With that he trudged off, shoulders drooping.

Having tidied her wagon, Adelia prepared to draw water from the creek for the stew pot. Concern over the unsolved thefts added to her worry for Siba and heartache over Gus. Something had to be done. She pulled the leather pouch from inside her dress and stared at it for several seconds as an idea formed in her mind.

She removed some of the gold, placing it in a tin can. Then she scooped up some cornmeal from the sack under her wagon and poured it into the bag with the gold dust. How like gold the yellow meal looked. She placed it atop her washstand where it was likely to be spotted easily and left her wagon. If someone made off with the bag while she was gone to the creek to draw water, she would be able to identify her gold

18

Mokelumne Hill, California
October 1849

Adelia walked slowly along the path to the creek, pulling her shawl tighter around her. The day would grow hot when the sun reached its zenith, but now the pre-autumn air sent a shiver through her. Perhaps it was more than the air that chilled her, for along this very path she had walked with Augustus only the day before.

She had tried to say that she didn't have time to walk and that she didn't want to hear any of his ready excuses. But her heart had been beating wildly, longing to experience again the tender touch of his hand, to hear the lovely lines that fell so easily from his lips. Or were they lovely lies? *My dear Miss Adelia Long, who has never been but a short step away from my heart during all my travels.*

When something stirred at her feet, she glanced down, half expecting to see the little covey of quail that had crossed their path yesterday. A lump caught in her throat as she recalled the moment Gus had stopped to admire them, catching her eye with a tenderness that left her breathless. But there were no quail, only a chipmunk that scampered past her feet and disappeared into the tall grass.

"Addie, wait up!"

Adelia turned to see Charity with Isaac at her side, each carrying a bucket. She had been so engrossed in thoughts of Augustus that she hadn't heard their approach.

"We've come to help you draw water for the cooking and washing," Charity said, waving her empty bucket in the air. She wore a calico dress with a pink sunbonnet that contrasted well with the dark hair hanging loose beneath it. Her cheeks were filling out and the gaunt figure softly rounding. "Hannibal went off before daybreak this morning, but I see he wasn't the only one up so early." She gave Adelia a knowing grin.

"With so many miners wanting breakfast, we have to start getting up before dawn," Adelia said, grateful for the distraction they provided. Charity had become a dear friend, and Isaac was a changed boy now that his mother was well.

"Hannibal says we've done so well that we may be able to go back on the wagon train coming through next month," she said. She lowered her head and fingered the bow beneath her chin. "I'm not sure I want to go." The words came softly, followed quickly by a warm hand on her arm. "Oh, Addie, I will miss you."

Adelia put a hand to her lips. She shouldn't be shocked. Others had left or were planning on returning, some with grand hopes for a new start among family and friends. Others, who had been less successful, were sick and weary of the demanding toil and were eager to bid farewell to the goldfields. What startled Adelia in that instant was the fact that she had no plan of her own. In the deepest recesses of her heart and mind, she had cherished a hope tied, if even by the thinnest thread, to Augustus Harte.

"We can write to each other," Charity offered, her eyes suddenly moist.

Adelia tried to reel in her desperate thoughts and check the tear that had begun making its way down her cheek. "Of course we will, Charity, but I shall miss you very much. Isaac too. I don't know what I would have done without you." More tears followed as Adelia's chin dropped to her chest.

"We would have been lost without *you*," Charity said quickly. "How I languished in my sorrow over my little Hannah, forgetting God's gracious gift of Isaac." She pulled the boy into her hip and hugged him hard. "And I'm not forgetting how you took care of us on the journey when sickness nearly overwhelmed us. You have a great gift, Addie."

She looked up in surprise.

"Why do you look so surprised?" Charity asked, laughing now. "Your knowledge of elixirs and herbs and such have kept half of us alive on this quest. Don't you know how much we all appreciate you? How much we owe you?"

Touched and humbled by her friend's words, Adelia fell silent.

"What do you think you and Quinton will do?" Charity asked abruptly. "Maybe you could go back with us when the train comes through."

Indeed, what lay ahead for her now? Coming west had been a great adventure from which she had learned much. She had been of service to others besides collecting enough money for a new start for herself and Quinton. But she hadn't thought seriously about going back to Iowa, back to Uncle Edward and Aunt Felicity, back to her station as an unmarried woman past her prime. She had loved the wide openheartedness of California, the opportunities that lay shining and real. Maybe they should make their home here.

But times were changing. People were changing. She longed for the early days, when hardship had bound their little mining community together, when everyone trusted their neighbor and had no need to guard their belongings. Greed was stealing the best in people and turning them into islands of desperation. She also recalled Gus's warning and Hoke's doubts about Wylie. Was it possible that he was behind all the thefts? Is that how he had made his fortune?

She knew what the love of money could do. She'd seen it in her own family who looked down on Papa because he wasn't successful in business and didn't own a fine home with the comforts money could buy. *"The love of money is the root of all evil."* That was what the Good Book said. It was inevitable, Adelia supposed, as competition grew for the best claims, that men would grow suspicious of one another and fight to gather more and more gold. All the while, gold lay not in shiny nuggets in the river nor on the ground but in friendships and the integrity of the heart.

"I—I don't know," Adelia responded, realizing that she had left Charity waiting too long for a reply. "I had thought—there was someone—" But she had hardened her heart toward him, and there was no going back.

Charity cocked her head. "The fine-looking gentleman you went walking with yesterday?"

Adelia turned a surprised eye.

"Secrets don't last long in a community like ours," Charity said. "I saw the way he looked at you. You with your fine light hair and eyes as deep and blue as a violet sea. You with a heart better than any gold California could offer." She filled her pail and wiped the droplets that had splashed on her face.

Adelia sighed. "Once we were—that is, I thought we might have a future together, but you see, he just picked up and left one day and never wrote or tried to find me—"

"Until yesterday."

"Yes. He said that shame kept him back. That he had to become rich before he could offer me anything." She stopped, hearing her distortion of Augustus's words. "Well," she said, drawing a deep breath, "it doesn't matter now. I said some very harsh things. I could not forgive him, and he—well, he probably can't forgive me now." Adelia stood abruptly, her bucket full and sloshing on the ground. "Let's get back. We've a lot of work to do." She smiled when Isaac took the bucket from her hand, insisting on carrying it for her.

On the walk back to camp, each was intent on private thoughts, and Adelia was glad there was no need to talk. If only she could quiet her heart and begin the slow work of forgetting Augustus Harte—again.

"I need to stop in my wagon before going to the cook tent," Adelia said when they had climbed the slope. "You can go on ahead if you want. I'll just be a minute."

She pressed the flap open and turned to the dressing table where she had left the pouch of gold mixed with cornmeal. It was gone. Her stomach lurched momentarily, but this was the test she was hoping for. She would demand that a search be made of every man's tent and shack, every poke and crock. How dare someone steal what they had all worked so hard and long for?

"Someone has stolen gold from my tent!" she hollered, jumping down from the wagon and catching up to Charity and Isaac. "Just this morning while we were at the creek." The news spread quickly as miners moved about the camp and began gathering at the cook tent.

"What's this all about?" Wylie Hunter appeared almost magically, peering down at her from astride his horse.

"My pouch of gold was on my dressing table this morning—only moments ago—and while I was drawing water, someone took it."

"I saw that thieving Injun!" Calvin Means hollered, stuffing into his belt a bottle from which he had been drinking. "He took my gold too, and my daddy's watch!"

Shouts of "Get that dirty Indian! Bring him in!" filtered from tent to tent and hung like smoke, choking the atmosphere.

Adelia stared in disbelief. She knew Siba had spent the night in the woods. Hoke had warned him to stay there. She believed he would not steal, especially not from her. Calvin was drunk or delirious or just being his hateful self. "Wait!" she screamed.

But Wylie and his band of vigilantes were not waiting for anything. "Mount up, men. Bring him in. We've had enough!"

"Pray, Charity," Adelia gasped as the mounted committee disappeared. *Why, oh why did I push the issue and set a trap? I should have known they would pin the thefts on Siba. That they wouldn't bother with investigating the theft.* "Oh, Charity," she moaned. "I wanted to catch the real thief, but I've put Siba's life in danger." She dropped down on the bench by the cook tent but sprang quickly to her feet again.

"Every tent and cabin must be searched," she announced in a flash of determination. *Including Wylie's,* she decided silently. Aloud, she told the group of puzzled miners crowding around her, "Everyone, please join in the search. Look for a pouch about this size." She held up her fingers to form its dimensions. "It has my mark—the letter *A* scratched into the leather on the bottom. I'm counting on you."

The remaining miners scattered, intent on their errand with crazed looks on their faces, and Adelia went directly to Wylie's tent and began unearthing everything, not thinking how angry he would be when he saw his belongings in disarray. She overturned everything, including his neatly made mattress. Aghast, she discovered beneath it numerous pokes and sacks filled with gold dust and nuggets. And, hastily stuffed in a corner, she found exactly what she was looking for—her pouch with the *A* scratched into the bottom. When Wylie had lifted it from her dressing table, he hadn't thought to look on the bottom. It was a pouch like a hundred others.

Removing her sunbonnet, she tucked the pouch carefully inside it, then tied it snugly around her waist. In only a matter of minutes, a thudding of human and animal feet shook Mok Hill. Adelia ran from the tent as a group of miners came charging up the slope, some on foot and some on horseback. The committee was returning. Gunshots rang out amid shouts of "Thief!" and "Dirty Injun!" along with a host of undistinguishable epithets.

Adelia's heart sank at the sight of Siba being pulled behind a pack mule, his hands tied together, a rope looped around his bare chest. Calvin Means had a rifle trained against his back.

Several miners converged on the scene, raising their fists and yelling for Siba's blood. "He had Calvin's watch hanging on his belt." Mild-mannered John Stoughton, red with rage, fumed as he yanked a rope from his saddle. Stumbling alongside the beleaguered Siba, he bellowed, "What are we waiting for? I say we string him up now!"

Adelia ran into the press of bodies, her eyes trained on a bewildered and struggling Siba. She pushed her way past sweaty bodies, heedless of shouts to stay back. "Don't be a fool! You want to be killed?" Wylie raved as he lumbered after her.

Mr. Stoughton was slinging a rope in the air, making several attempts before looping it over Siba's head. Two other miners tugged at the rope still wound around the victim's chest and wrists, which were torn and bleeding from the extreme pressure of being pulled up the hill.

"Get him up!" Someone yelled, and two men hoisted Siba onto the back of a snorting steed that reared wildly, eyes glassy with fear.

"Stop!" Adelia screamed into the melee. She fought her way forward to the stand of oak trees where Siba was being dragged. "Stop! In the name of God and all that's decent, don't do this."

Calvin Means stumbled, and his rifle exploded in the air. The sound of the gunshot served to halt the crowd momentarily, and they all turned to stare at her, a fine lady with flowing blond hair and billowing skirt flinging herself into the whirling maelstrom.

"My daddy's watch was hanging on his belt!" Calvin Means shouted. "He took it from my tent when he stole my gold. The dirty Indian took it sure!"

Adelia kept her voice clear and steady. "Siba, is this true?"

"I did not steal," Siba rasped, struggling for breath. "I found the watch downriver when I dug for gold. I did not know where it came from. I did not steal this man's gold."

"I've seen that watch on your belt, Calvin Means," Adelia said, drawing herself up as tall as she could and looking him straight in the eye. "You've been showing it off and bragging on it, especially after you've been drinking."

"That's right!" Quinton hollered at Means, breaching the crowd to stand next to Siba. "You had that watch on your chain when you headed out of camp. I saw it."

"You lost it yourself at the diggings," Adelia said. "Siba merely picked it up. Wouldn't you?"

"Besides, everybody knows that Indians have no use for gold," Quinton charged in a voice full of irony. "They work for food, right? Some of you have taken advantage of this man's labor and given almost nothing in return."

A number of the miners looked down shamefacedly, knowing Quinton's words were true. Still, quieter grumbles of "Worthless Injun" and "No good red thief" issued from the pack.

Adelia pushed a finger in Calvin Means's chest. "You have no proof that he took any gold from your tent." Calvin drew a meaty hand across his mouth and stared at her through bloodshot eyes. But he said nothing. The others, equally stunned, shuffled their feet and grumbled under their breath.

"The committee will handle this!" came the roaring voice of Wylie Hunter, who had pushed forward and now stood a few paces from her. "Hold him there!" he demanded. Several pairs of hands descended on Siba. He was held firmly in the saddle, his hands still bound and bleeding.

"I think not!" Adelia shouted with more force than she knew she possessed. "Siba is not the thief. While you were chasing that poor man, we searched every miner's tent. I had the right, since it was my gold most recently taken."

"Get out of the way!" Wylie shouted, dismounting and slapping his horse on the flank. "I'm in charge of this committee, and we will have justice."

Adelia advanced until she was nose to nose with Wylie. Then, ripping the laden sunbonnet from her waist, she held up the pouch of gold she had recovered from his tent. "Indeed, we will have justice. I just found this in *your* tent, Mr. Hunter. You're the thief. *You!*"

Wylie's ruddy face went white. "How dare you?"

"I deliberately left it in sight in my wagon to catch the thief." She held it aloft, waving it back and forth for the benefit of everyone watching. "See, my mark is scratched into the bottom."

"She's lying!" Wylie yelled, looking about at the angry faces now turned to him. "She put it in my tent just to save her precious Indian."

"Not so," Hannibal Reed intoned, drawing himself up to his full six-foot height. Next to him, Charity pointed her finger at Wylie. "Adelia mixed cornmeal in with her gold to trap the thief." She held out her hand for Adelia to pour a bit of the mixture into her palm. "Look. Test it on your tongue."

Several of the miners poked their fingers into her palm and touched them to their lips. Hoke put his finger in and let out a roar. "Best-tasting gold I ever ate!"

"And check his tent!" Adelia cried. "You'll find all of your missing gold beneath his mattress."

The miners had always trusted Adelia. They viewed her as something of an angel of mercy who cared for the sick and by her very presence and bearing reminded them of loved ones far away. Now they quickly rose to her defense, bellowing angrily at Wylie, their faces hard with anger.

"Release the Indian!" someone shouted, and Siba's bands were cut and the rope removed from his neck.

In one swift move of his left hand, Wylie whipped his pistol from his belt. With his other hand, he pulled Adelia against his chest. "Shoot me, and she gets it!" he shouted to the mass of men heading toward him. Eyes wild, he began edging Adelia toward the wooded perimeter of the camp.

"You hurt her, and I'll hunt you down!" yelled Quinton, pushing into the crowd and pounding toward Wylie. "There's nowhere you'll be safe."

Adelia's heart pounded. Wylie held her fast by her waist, crushing her arms against his body. *Is this where the madness will end? For a handful of gold shall I lose my life and a man his soul?*

Suddenly a tall, blond-haired man leaped from the trees, grabbed Wylie's gun arm, and yanked him backward. Adelia jumped away as a shot rang out wildly.

Augustus Harte pummeled the helpless Wylie to the ground until he couldn't rise as angry men rushed to Wylie, guns pointed at the fallen man. "No!" Gus shouted. "Hasn't there been enough killing in this land?"

"Yes," Adelia joined, "we will have our gold back, and this man will never be able to show his face on Mok Hill again."

When the crowd had quieted and Wylie Hunter had been "escorted" from the camp, she turned to Augustus. "How did you know?" she asked weakly.

"Did you think I'd leave you in the hands of that deserter?" he said, drawing an arm across her shoulders and pulling her gently into his chest. "He abandoned our troops in '48 before the surrender of Mexico. He's been a curse on the land ever since."

He paused to take a breath. "If they don't kill him on the way, he'll be long gone from Mok Hill, and you'll never be bothered by him again."

"Augustus . . . Gus," she began, whispering against his chest. "I'm sorry. I—I hoped you would come back, but I didn't think you would after the way I treated you."

"Hush, my dear Miss Long," he said huskily. "However long the road may be, it's only a short step from my heart to yours. Adelia, dear Addie, don't you know how much I love you?"

19

Cabot Falls, Vermont
Present Day

"So it was one of your art students after all?" Rosa, poised and elegant, folded her hands in her lap. Her dark eyes were filled with admiration for Sofia.

The whole family, along with Marla and Julie, was gathered in the four-season room with the kids chattering noisily and bouncing in and out. Jim served drinks and hors d'oeuvres with a white towel laid over his arm butler style. He held out a tray of bruschetta and crostini to Sofia and gave her a lingering wink.

"How did you know?" Gina asked. She leaned into Sofia on the couch and linked arms with her sister.

"Ernest tipped his own hand," Sofia said. "We only suspected he could be the one after Marla found a connection to Wylie Hunter. Julie spent hours in the library too, looking for names and dates tied to the Gold Rush."

"And it was the diary he was really after?" Rosa asked.

"He was so afraid the world would learn about what his forebears had done—that his family's reputation and his own would be ruined. He had been drinking before coming over and was in no state to be reasoned with. I never should have opened the door, but I was fortunate to have someone watching out for me."

She had told everyone several times how Jim had left the car with Vanessa and asked a friend to take him home. How he had put his key in the lock at just the right moment. "No way was I going to be far away with you home alone," he had told her later. "Not while these crazy things have been happening. I just wanted to make sure the kids got safely to the game." Sofia gave Jim a loving glance. Having Officer Quimby on the lookout hadn't been enough for her watchful husband.

"If Mr. Haynes had just kept quiet, it never would have come out that his great-grandfather had an infamous past," Rosa said thoughtfully.

"And even if it had been revealed, people wouldn't blame him for something someone else did," Sofia said quietly. "He should have known you can't deny history." She sighed. "You can deny it, I guess, but you can't change it. We're only responsible for what we do with our own lives. It's up to us to live honestly and well, no matter what our past might be."

Vanessa, ever the champion of the vulnerable, had been moved to hear of Haynes's desperation. "What will happen to him?" she asked.

"Yeah, will he have to do jail time, Mom?" Luke put in, blue eyes serious.

"Well," she said slowly, "we have the pouch back. I don't think pressing charges against Ernest will serve any good purpose. I know he hired that young man to break into our house and later to follow me—"

Jim whirled around aghast. "Someone was following you?"

"I wasn't sure at the time," Sofia explained. She had been right about the dark sedan, and Haynes had admitted he'd put the man on her tail the day she stopped at the coffee shop. "I began to think it was just me being paranoid. And I didn't want to worry you. That's why I didn't say anything." She gave Jim an apologetic smile and hoped he could read the love in her eyes. "It was the same amateur who tried to break in last week. Someone Ernest got to do his dirty work." She shook her head. "He must have been desperate. I can't help feeling sorry for him."

"That's pretty serious stuff," Jim said, frowning. "Besides, he broke in here and pushed you around."

"Yes, but he didn't hurt me. And you came in just at the right time." She paused and gave him a lingering look. "You've always been here for me—for all of us."

Quiet ensued for a long moment, and then Rosa spoke. "Do you think Adelia Long wrote those words herself—about gold making 'fools of us all'?"

"We think it's likely," Sofia answered. "It looks a lot like the writing in the diary. As for those two capital letters on the tag that we thought were *V* and *N*, we think they actually are *W. H.*—for Wylie Hunter. He was stealing gold from the other miners at Mok Hill and covering his thefts by pretending to preserve law and order."

"So the gold and the pouch are authentic," Julie exclaimed, her green eyes alight with excitement.

"The authorities are still examining it, but they think so. Especially if the scratching on the bottom turns out to form an *A*. It just looked like scuff marks to us. Then Ernest took the pouch before we had time to study it."

"So are we rich now?" Matthew asked.

Sofia smiled and tousled his curly head. "The pouch will go to the historical society, where its true value and the lessons of the Gold Rush can be appreciated by everyone. The gold itself may be worth about five hundred dollars. The rest of the bag contains gravel and sediment—and the cornmeal Adelia mixed in deliberately to catch the thief, whose initials she wrote on the tag later."

"Clever girl, our Adelia Long," Jim said.

"Yes, she deserved to find happiness with Gus." Sofia lifted a folded paper from the coffee table. It was a photocopy of a newspaper column. She and Marla had guessed that the couple would marry, that they might return to Iowa or Minnesota or remain in California. It was in the *Kanesville Chronicle* for May 1853 that they found the reference to the marriage of Miss Adelia Rose Long and Mr. Augustus Langley Harte.

Sofia cleared her throat, commanding everyone's attention while she read, "'The couple, who returned from California by overland coach this spring, will settle in Kanesville, where Mr. Harte plans to open a haberdashery on Lincoln Street.'"

Everyone applauded.

"Kanesville became Council Bluffs," Sofia said. "It was a real jumping-off place for people heading to California. And a great many people did. We know that the Gold Rush was one of the most significant events to shape American history during the first half of the nineteenth century."

"It sure changed California," Jim said.

"It changed a lot of people," Sofia said quietly. "Nothing good comes from loving money. Real treasure lies within the heart. It's found in doing the right thing, even when it's hard, and cherishing your family and friends."

They were quiet for a few moments, absorbed in their thoughts. Then Rosa stood and held out her glass. "I propose a toast," she said. "To that clever Adelia Long—and to Sofia, the best and wisest sister anyone could have."

"Hear, hear!" Gina pronounced, leaning in to press her cheek against Sofia's. "To Sofia, a real treasure."

Learn more about Annie's fiction books at

AnniesFiction.com

We've designed the Annie's Fiction website especially for you!

Access your e-books • Read sample chapters • Manage your account

Choose from one of these great series:

Amish Inn Mysteries

Annie's Attic Mysteries

Annie's Mysteries Unraveled

Annie's Quilted Mysteries

Annie's Secrets of the Quilt

Antique Shop Mysteries

Chocolate Shoppe Mysteries

Creative Woman Mysteries

Hearts of Amish Country

Secrets of the Castleton Manor Library

Victorian Mansion Flower Shop Mysteries

What are you waiting for? Visit us now at **AnniesFiction.com!**